"You Think They Expect Us To Sleep Together?"

He tilted his head and held her gaze.

"Probably, yes." She nodded.

He lifted a brow. Heat flared in his groin. "Do you think we should?"

Her cheek heated under his thumb. "Yes, I do." Her voice was low, breathy.

AJ blinked. He'd not expected that answer. In fact, he'd had no intention of doing more than kissing her.

But since he was a healthy male, he rose from the sofa and took her hand. "Then I guess we'd better go into the bedroom."

Dear Reader,

This story is the first of three books about Royal Rebels, strong men already successful in their chosen field, who find themselves unexpectedly thrust onto the throne of their ancestral homeland.

The germ of inspiration for the series came when the Harlequin Desire editors asked me to write *Prince of Midtown,* in 2008. I'm not sure I'd have ever considered writing a royal of my own accord—I'm a big fan of democracy—but I loved the process of creating my energetic and charming prince and his romantic Mediterranean homeland.

The enthusiastic reader mail I received for that book made it clear that there's something irresistible about a royal hero. Perhaps it's the limitless wealth, and the power and influence beyond most of our wildest dreams. Or maybe the sense of honor that comes with accepting duties you've been born to. Either way, I couldn't resist writing more royal heroes.

This first story takes place in the palm-shaded island of Rahiri, where I had fun creating a lush Pacific paradise for my king to rule along with his lovely queen—if they can just find their way to that happy ending. I hope you enjoy AJ and Lani's story.

Jen

JENNIFER LEWIS

THE PRINCE'S PREGNANT BRIDE

Recycling programs
for this product may
not exist in your area.

ISBN-13: 978-0-373-73095-7

THE PRINCE'S PREGNANT BRIDE

Copyright © 2011 by Jennifer Lewis

Printed in U.S.A.

Books by Jennifer Lewis

Desire

The Boss's Demand #1812
Seduced for the Inheritance #1830
Black Sheep Billionaire #1847
Prince of Midtown #1891
*Millionaire's Secret Seduction #1925
*In the Argentine's Bed #1931
*The Heir's Scandalous Affair #1938
The Maverick's Virgin Mistress #1977
The Desert Prince #1993
Bachelor's Bought Bride #2012
†The Prince's Pregnant Bride #2082

*The Hardcastle Progeny
†Royal Rebels

JENNIFER LEWIS

has been dreaming up stories for as long as she can remember and is thrilled to be able to share them with readers. She has lived on both sides of the Atlantic and worked in media and the arts before she grew bold enough to put pen to paper. Happily settled in England with her family, she would love to hear from readers at jen@jenlewis.com. Visit her website at www.jenlewis.com.

For Sue, my fun and generous friend and neighbor,
who helps make living here such a pleasure.

Acknowledgments:

Many thanks to the lovely people who read this book
while I was writing it—Anne, Cynthia, Jerri, Leeanne,
my agent Andrea and my editor Charles.

One

"What do you mean I *have* to marry her?" AJ Rahia tried to keep his voice down. Waiters passed out champagne, and the polite hum of conversation buzzed in his ears. The woman in question stood only a few yards away, in the well-dressed crowd of mourners at the wake.

His mother took his hand between her two soft ones. "It's your duty. If the king dies, one of his brothers must marry the royal widow."

The carved walls of the old palace seemed to close in on him. "That's ridiculous. It's the twenty-first century. And I'm sure she doesn't want to marry me any more than I want to marry her." He resisted the urge to turn and glance at the petite young widow he hadn't even seen since her wedding five years earlier.

His mother tilted her head and spoke softly. "She's as sweet as she is beautiful."

"Mom!"

"And I have no other sons."

AJ stiffened. Something had happened during his own birth that left his mom unable to have more children. Just another burden of guilt that settled uncomfortably back on his shoulders each time he returned to Rahiri.

He'd just arrived for his brother's funeral—or whatever you called it when there was no body—and already his ticket back to L.A. was burning a hole in his pocket.

"I'm sure she'll want to mourn for at least a year before she thinks about marrying again." He rested his hand on his mom's shoulder. She was so tiny. Or he was so huge. He resisted a powerful urge to hug this very demanding but fiercely loving woman. "Then you'll find the perfect husband for her."

"You can't *choose* a king." His mother looked up, her eyes imploring. "A king is born."

"And I wasn't born to be king. Most people are convinced I was born to direct big-budget action movies, which is why they give me so much money for it."

His mom waved her hand, dismissive. "Child's play and you know it." She took his hand and squeezed it between her palms. "Come home. You belong here, and we need you."

He ignored the tightening in his chest. "To rule the country? I don't think so. How about Cousin Ainu? He's always trying to run everything. He'd be thrilled."

His mom narrowed her eyes, which caused her mascaraed lashes to clump together. "The Rahia family has ruled Rahiri for as long as anyone can remember. That chain of tradition cannot be broken."

"Change can be good." He didn't sound as convincing

as he'd hoped. "Out with the old, in with the..." He stopped in horror as his mom's usually sharp black eyes filled with tears. "I'm sorry, that was insensitive of me. I didn't mean that Vanu's death was...was..."

A good thing?

Though it had been his first thought when he'd heard the news.

On the other hand, if he was suddenly expected to fill his brother's narrow designer shoes, it was a very bad thing.

"I know, sweetheart. You can't help speaking your thoughts. You were always like that, wild, free-spirited—"

"And totally unsuitable to be a monarch."

He wasn't quite such a wild child as his reputation suggested, but the image could work in his favor now.

"Come talk to Lani." His mom's lipsticked smile did nothing to mask the steely determination in her eyes. AJ glanced around. Hopefully none of the gathered mourners had any idea of her intentions. Especially his brother's widow.

She pulled him across the room with a pincer grip on his hand, pink nails digging into his flesh. "Lani, dear, you remember AJ? Vanu's younger brother."

Panic flashed in the young woman's eyes. "Y-yes," she stammered. "Yes, of course I do. Pleased to meet you again." A forced smile quivered on her lips.

She knew.

And was horrified.

AJ extended his hand and shook hers. Her fingers trembled against his palm. Small and slight, she was wrapped in a traditional blue mourning dress, partially covered by her long, loose hair. He'd remembered her unusual eyes—gold-brown, like polished tortoise-shell—but not the haunted look in them.

"I'm so sorry for your loss." He glanced away from her face, which was polite in Rahiian tradition. And good advice in any case because Lani Rahia was an extraordinary beauty.

Clear, fine features mingled her Rahiian and American heritage. Her skin glowed like the proverbial milk and honey. Her thick, lustrous hair looked brown in ordinary light, but if touched by sunshine it shone brilliantly as pure, twenty-four carat gold.

He could see why his brother—or was it his mother who had truly chosen her?—had picked Lani as queen despite her humble background.

But he had no intention of being her king.

Lani pulled her hand back fast and wiped it on her dress before she could stop herself. That handshake was supposed to preface intimacies that made her stomach turn.

She was expected to marry this man simply because he was her husband's younger brother.

At least he had the good grace not to stare her in the eyes the way most Americans thought normal. He wasn't American, of course, but she felt too fragile to meet anyone's gaze for long. He'd lived in L.A. the entire time she'd been at the palace.

Taller than his brother, she noticed. And broader, too. In the glimpse she'd caught of his face he looked kind.

But she knew only too well that appearances could be deceptive.

"Vanu's disappearance must have been a terrible shock." The deep voice hung in the air, since it took a moment for Lani to emerge from her frenzied thoughts to realize he'd spoken.

"Oh, yes. Terrible. He went out late one night—to think, he said—and he never came back."

She'd lain in bed, shaking with terror, waiting for him to return and "finish the job." He'd said he would, with that cruel hiss in his voice and a cold gleam in his eyes. The hours had ticked by as she awaited her doom.

Then the sun rose, and the birds started to sing.

"It must be so hard not knowing what happened." She heard compassion in AJ's voice. What kind of name was AJ? She didn't even know his real Rahiian name. No one ever called him by it.

"We still don't know what happened." Lani's mother-in-law dabbed at her eyes with a handkerchief. "But after ninety days—" She pressed a muffled sob into the linen. "A successor must be chosen."

Lani stiffened. According to Rahiian tradition, the successor would take her as his wife. Presumably the tradition existed to provide protection for the children of royal widows and avoid jostling for succession between children and siblings of the late king. But she didn't have any children.

"Ninety days...that's still at least a month away. Who would normally succeed, if the king had no siblings?" AJ asked his mother.

She dabbed at her eyes. "Impossible. The king always has siblings. The ability to bear many children is a Rahiian blessing." She coughed a sob into her handkerchief.

Lani glanced at AJ, whose brow furrowed with distress. "Mom, don't upset yourself. Please. We'll get it all figured out. Don't you worry."

He slid his big arm around his mother's back and rubbed her shoulder. Lani felt a flush of warmth at the kind gesture.

"Thank you, sweetheart." His mother smiled at AJ. "Why don't you take Lani out on the veranda for a rest? I'm sure she's exhausted after the funeral and having to talk with all these people."

The big man glanced at Lani. She swallowed. She'd rather be here in this frying pan of semi-strangers than alone, in private, with her...future husband.

Surely they wouldn't make her go through with it?

"Would you like to, er..." He extended his arm, inviting her to take it.

Lani fought the urge to recoil and reached her fingers up to his. His forearm was thickly muscled, not hard and wiry like her husband's—her late husband's. Her skin tingled with awareness—or was it terror?—as she slid her arm into his.

He cleared his throat. "Please excuse us." He nodded to her mother.

"Of course." His mother's smile broadened as she no doubt saw her plans moving one step closer to completion.

Lani tried to maintain a neutral expression as they walked slowly across the room together. Did all these people expect her to marry this man? Were they eagerly looking for signs of fresh commitment when her husband was barely cold in his grave?

Technically he wasn't in a grave at all, since they'd never found a body. Or his boat.

"Sorry about my mother," AJ murmured as they stepped out into a cool, empty hallway. His voice echoed slightly off the white stone floor. AJ pulled back his arm, and hers fell to her side. A small blue parrot stared at them from his perch in the latticework.

"She's just doing what she thinks is best." She glanced at him, trying to gauge his feelings.

"Do you think it's for the best?" He frowned, and peered at her. His eyes were a warm dark brown, like polished teak.

"I don't know." Her voice came out a choked whisper. "I'm inexperienced in these matters." And not about to defy a thousand years of royal tradition in the face of a Rahiian prince. If he was anything like his brother, he'd let her know his disapproval in the harshest terms possible.

"You're a grown woman. Do you think it's natural to marry a total stranger?"

His question embarrassed her. "I only met Vanu three times before I married him."

"Let me guess, my mom fixed up the whole thing." He raised a straight black brow.

Lani nodded. Her long hair felt hot on the back of her neck and she wished she could run to her room for a good cry.

And not over the death—or supposed death—of her husband. For herself, and the no-win situation she faced: another unhappy royal marriage, or disgrace and dishonor for refusing it. Tears pricked her eyes and she raised a hand to cover them.

"Please don't cry." AJ's gruff plea rang off the wood-beamed ceiling. "Come on, let's go sit on the veranda. Some fresh air will do us both good."

His words were supposed to be funny, since the hall they walked along was open to the gardens, like nearly every room in the sprawling palace. Carved wood cast shade and the high roof kept out tropical rain, but birds and pretty lizards darted freely amongst the ornate columns.

Yet the air itself seemed oppressive, thick with expectation.

AJ Rahia was tall, well over six feet, and her head barely reached his shoulders. Her small steps, bound by the long wrap of her skirt, made her scurry to keep up with his bold strides. He noticed, and stopped to wait for her.

He wore a dark suit, American-style, and must have been hot in the tropical humidity. "Would you like a cool drink?" She lowered her eyes, not wanting him to hear any hint of suggestion beyond mere politeness.

"No, thanks. Listen, it's not personal. I'm sure you're a very nice girl. I've just got a life in the States. I direct movies—"

"I know," she rushed. "Your mother is very proud. She watches the whole *Dragon Chaser* series at least once a month."

He stopped dead. "You're kidding."

"Not at all. She installed a complete home theater system in the old feasting chamber last year for better stereo sound."

AJ's eyes widened. "She's never said a word."

"She's a big fan." Lani couldn't help the tiny smile that sneaked across her mouth. He looked so totally astonished. "She loves the lead actor, too. She thinks he's cute."

"Devi Anderson? Cute!" AJ burst out into a loud guffaw. "I swear, nothing could surprise me more. Well…" His brows lowered. "Except that I'm expected to marry you."

Lani swallowed. She lifted her hair off her neck and rearranged it down her back, her eyes glued to the floor.

Should she apologize for being a burden? It was hardly her fault.

And he might take it the wrong way.

He didn't look anything like his brother, but that didn't mean he didn't share the same twisted soul. That he wouldn't lash out when she least expected it.

"Sorry, I shouldn't keep bringing it up." He frowned and turned away. "It's just so…ridiculous. And I have a big investor meeting on Tuesday I must get back for."

A tiny flame of hope lit in Lani's chest. He really didn't plan to stay and marry her. He obviously didn't want to. She should be offended, but instead she felt relief.

Even if she didn't believe in true love any more, she'd had enough of marriage for one lifetime.

They'd reached the veranda, where big armchairs nestled under palm fronds with a view over the forested Haialia valley. They sat in two chairs separated by a carved-wood table.

"What do you think happened to Vanu?" AJ turned to look at her.

She shrank from his inquisitive gaze. "One of the boats went missing from the palace dock. A small yacht he used to sail sometimes. Some say he might have taken it out. There was a storm that night." She swallowed. Images of Vanu disappearing into the dark sea crowded her brain.

"If there was a storm the boat could have broken free by itself. They do that quite often. The palace dock isn't well protected." AJ wove his long fingers together and looked out over the valley.

"I know, but the island isn't that big and everyone's been searching for him for weeks. He must have left."

She bit her lip. "And he didn't take a plane. They're all accounted for."

"Why did he go out in a storm?" AJ's eyes rested on her cheek.

Which heated. No one could know the truth. Her marriage was over now and there was no reason for anyone to know that it had been...hell on earth.

She owed that much to her mother-in-law, who'd done everything to welcome her as a daughter and who worshipped and loved her eldest son.

"I think he was restless. Couldn't sleep." She fixed her eyes on the horizon, where rainforest haze hung just above the treetops. "He often walked in the gardens late at night. He didn't sleep much."

"Yeah. He was like that as a boy, too. It sometimes seemed like he never slept."

An odd tone in AJ's voice made her glance at him. His brow was furrowed in a frown. He must miss Vanu, the older brother he'd never see again.

AJ's face was undeniably handsome, with broad, well-cut cheekbones and a slightly cleft chin. His mouth was wide and friendly. So different from his brother's pinched, bony countenance.

She'd married Vanu because she had to. That's what everyone said. What simple village girl—the daughter of a laundress, no less—would turn down a chance to be queen?

She didn't have a good answer at the time.

"How's my mom taking it?" AJ's frown deepened.

"Very hard." Lani twisted her fingers together. "She cries a lot, and that's not like her."

"It's a terrible thing to lose a child." AJ rubbed a hand over his mouth. "At least she has you. I know she adores you."

Lani pushed a smile to her lips. "She's been so kind to me. Everyone has."

Well, except Vanu.

"So if I take off back to L.A., I imagine you'll rule as queen."

Lani sat bolt upright. "Me? I can't. I'm not royal."

"You may not have been born royal, but you're already queen, in case you hadn't noticed." Humor danced in his dark eyes.

"Technically speaking, but not really. I'm just a village girl."

"I thought you were born in New Jersey." He raised a brow.

"My parents divorced when I was seven, and my mom moved back to Rahiri." People tried to make more than they should of her foreign birth and the fact that she was half-American. It gave her unusual features and coloring, nothing more.

"You seem more educated than the average village girl." His penetrating gaze made her belly tighten.

"We have good schools here. Your father saw to that when he was king. Many of our teachers received scholarships to study abroad, and brought their knowledge back to Rahiri."

"But your father's a professor, isn't he?" AJ leaned closer, until his masculine scent tickled her nostrils.

What was he trying to prove?

"Of geology. He encouraged me in my studies, and I was going to read history at the university, but I left my studies when I became queen."

Vanu hadn't liked to see her with her head in a book. He said such a pretty head should be completely empty.

"You should start again. Why not?" He shrugged.

"I never had the patience for school. I'm at my best running around on a set."

"You're happy in L.A.?"

"Ecstatically so. I can honestly say I don't miss Rahiri one bit."

"Your mom misses you."

"I know. That's why she comes up with so many excuses for shopping trips to Rodeo Drive." He grinned. "I enjoy her visits and I think she single-handedly keeps the U.S. economy afloat."

"Is this your first visit to Rahiri since the wedding?"

"Yes. Maybe I should feel bad, but I'm busy and I don't fit in here." He pushed a hand through his thick black hair and leaned back in the woven armchair. The heavy muscling of his body was visible even inside his dark suit.

She was still surprised that he hadn't visited once. And they expected him to become king?

Not very likely. Which meant she was off the hook as his wife.

She blew out a long, slow, silent breath. The sooner he left, the better.

"It is beautiful here, though." He stared out at the mist-shrouded horizon, a crevice of gold and blue sky nestled between rainforest-covered hills. A toucan flew up into a nearby baobab tree, its bright beak held aloft. "I'd forgotten how beautiful it is."

His mom's quest to convince him to stay continued unrelentingly over the following days and nights.

"Here, sweetheart, have some coconut stars." Her favorite treat hovered under AJ's nose on their tooled silver platter.

"No, thanks, Mom, really." After three days of funerary feasting, he wasn't sure he'd ever be able to eat again. "Did I tell you my plane leaves at 6:00 a.m. tomorrow?"

"What?" Her eyes widened with horror. "You can't. You've barely had time to get to know Lani."

He glanced around, making sure the woman in question was nowhere nearby. "I've spent hours and hours with her. She's sweet."

"And she'll be a good queen, with you as her king." His mom folded her arms. Her gold bangles clinked together.

"Not possible."

"Not only is it possible, it is inevitable." Steel shimmered in his mom's voice and gleamed in her eyes. "Although it took a tragedy to bring you together, you and Lani are destined to be together."

"I'm destined to begin post-production on *Hellcat Four: The Aftermath* in three weeks' time. And after that, if the funding comes together, I'll be making *Dragon Chaser* part five."

His mom waved her hand, jangling her bracelets. "Part four, part five. What will it matter if there are so many already? There is only one Rahiri, and you are our ruler."

"People are counting on me. There's a lot at stake."

"My sentiments exactly." She leaned in, giving him a whiff of her familiar honeysuckle perfume. "We're all counting on you. I am counting on you."

AJ's back tightened. No one here had counted on him for anything before. He wasn't the heir, the chosen one. Now suddenly everything had changed, but he was still the same person inside.

His mom grabbed his arm. "Here comes Lani. Don't tell her you're leaving. You're not leaving."

AJ jerked his arm back. "I'm leaving. But I'll be nice to Lani before I go."

He smiled at the stunning young widow as she walked into the room, her embroidered pale-gold dress gleaming in the candlelight. Gold earrings glittered in her lobes and a ruby hovered at her throat. Decked out for sacrifice.

His stomach turned that she was so willing to go along with his mother's foolish plot. Did she have no spine? Did she want no say in the choice of her future husband?

"Hey, Lani."

"Hello, AJ." Her head dipped slightly, deferential, which annoyed him all the more. He liked women with some spunk, some fire.

"Come with me." He threaded his arm though hers and led her from the room. Away from his mother's anxious ears.

He ignored a flicker of heat from the touch of his skin against hers. He could not possibly be attracted to this shrinking violet barely out of another man's arms.

They walked through a high doorway and out into a palace courtyard ringed with potted palms. "You're too nice, you know."

"I...I..." Her hesitation irked him further.

"Can't you say anything for yourself, can't you speak your mind?" His growl startled her.

She glanced up, honey-colored eyes wide. Was she afraid of him?

"I'm sorry." She bit her full, pink lip. A flash of heat to his groin sent a surge of fury through AJ. Just because she had a pretty face did not mean she'd make a good wife. Maybe she deserved to be married off to some stranger.

A silky lock of gold-hued hair fell forward as she hung her head.

He had no interest in how that hair would feel under his palms, or trailing over his chest as she crouched over him, maybe panting slightly, golden eyes wide with desire.

Because that would never happen.

He scowled and turned away. "I'm flying out tomorrow. You're on your own, sister."

"What?" Her voice rang across the room, high and breathless.

He spun around to face her. "You heard me. I'm done playing my part in this charade. You and I have nothing whatsoever in common, and I have no intention of sacrificing both our lives on the altar of Rahiian tradition. I'm going back to my real life."

She blinked, speechless. Hardly a surprise. She didn't have much to say for herself at the best of times. But her cheeks reddened. "You dislike me."

Her words sent a fist of guilt to AJ's gut. She hadn't actually done anything wrong, after all. She'd been trying so hard to be a sweet Rahiian maiden.

Shame he couldn't stand sweet Rahiian maidens.

Her ruby shone bloodred at her throat. Set in an ornate gold setting, the royal jewel had probably been worn by many sacrificial lambs before her. He pitied and despised these women, so ready to give their whole lives to the service of a man. For a country that didn't care if they lived or died.

He stared down at her—she barely came up to his shoulder—and cocked his head. "You're too…nice."

"I'm not nice at all. Really." The words rushed out. Was she so afraid of failing in her royal duty? "I mean, I try to be, but…"

Words failed her once again. The pink flush of her cheeks gave the inappropriate impression that she was aroused. Her lips, parted in protest, looked full and ripe, ready for kissing. The look in her eyes, glossy with terror, could easily be mistaken for a gaze shimmering with need. Desire crept over him like the tropical heat, uncoiling in his belly, unfurling along with his fury over this crazy situation.

For once he wanted this girl to give him an honest reaction. He was letting her down. Screwing her over. Just once he wanted to hear her words ring harsh in the air, sense her anger pulse on the night breeze, or maybe even feel that small hand slap him hard across the face.

Then maybe he wouldn't feel so guilty.

Surely she had a dark side. Everyone did.

He took a step forward, pulled her into his arms and crushed his mouth over hers.

For a second Lani froze, and he half braced for her reaction.

Then her arms stretched around his back and her slim body molded to his. Her mouth softened, opened to welcome his kiss. Her fingers dug into the muscles of his back and drew him closer, until her breasts crushed against his chest.

Surprise and sharp lust flashed through AJ. Lani was kissing him back—hard. Her breath came in unsteady gasps. Heat pulsed between them, urging their heartbeats into a fevered dance. A tiny moan quivered in

Lani's throat as he thickened against her, his desire provoking a fierce arousal.

This was *not* the response he'd expected.

Two

He pulled away first. Lani's hand flew to her lips, left suddenly cold and bare. She didn't want to open her eyes but she forced herself. AJ's dark gaze fixed on hers, wide with—shock.

What just happened?

He'd initiated the kiss, his action deliberate, forceful even. But she couldn't shake the impression that he hadn't wanted to kiss her.

Her lips still stung and tingled with stray pulses of energy. Her nipples pressed against the crisp fabric of her dress, above her pounding heart. The hand now pressed against her mouth—hot with her own unsteady breaths—had just a moment ago been fisted into his shirt, clutching at his thick muscles.

Shame flushed through her in a hot wave. He must have kissed her out of a sense of responsibility, to prove he could step into the role everyone expected of him, whether he liked it or not.

And she'd responded in a way that was anything but dutiful.

Was she going mad? She gulped. Her body felt hot, thick with unfamiliar sensation. She couldn't bring herself to glance at AJ again. He hadn't moved an inch since he'd pushed her away.

He'd had to push her away, to stop her clinging closer and tighter, pressing his body to hers with a fierce grip. At her own husband's funeral.

Or whatever you called a funeral without a body.

She must be mad. There was no other explanation. Should she apologize? Anger flashed inside her. He'd taken the kiss—stolen it—so anything it led to was his fault.

Still, no one would have expected her to respond with…desperation.

He'd thought she was too nice. Now he knew she was anything but.

Her face heated and she glanced up. AJ shoved a hand through his thick, black hair. His lips parted, but he didn't speak.

I'm sorry. The words hovered on her tongue for a single instant—automatic, a learned response—before she swallowed them, bitter and tasteless. She didn't owe him an apology. She didn't owe her late husband one, either, for that matter. These powerful men took what they wanted, without a thought for those they took them from. Which is why she didn't want to marry again— especially not another Rahia.

Her treacherous thoughts pounded in her brain like a headache. If he knew what she was thinking he'd…

Lani gathered her skirt and rushed for the door.

* * *

AJ stared after Lani as her gold dress disappeared through the carved archway. He hadn't said anything to stop her, since he couldn't think of what to say. He had no idea what to even think. If his mom knew they'd shared such a steamy kiss, she'd probably be over the moon. Or would she be scandalized that it had happened before the funeral feasts were even finished?

He blew out a hard blast of air. He'd expected her to squeal and slap him. To defend her virtue and hurl angry words in his face. To hate him.

Which was his intention. Then she wouldn't want him to do his duty and marry her. He'd be off the hook.

Instead she'd seemed to…enjoy the kiss.

He shook his head, trying to shake loose a sensible thought. Maybe she'd faked it. As a royal wife—especially his brother's wife—she must have had plenty of practice faking pleasure when she didn't feel it.

Still…

The way her fingers had clawed at his back. How her mouth had opened to welcome his, her sweet breath hot on his tongue. He'd even heard a tiny moan, like the cry of a bird, newly uncaged, escape her throat before he came to his senses and pulled back.

His stiff suit barely hid the reaction she'd provoked in his body. His blood seemed ten degrees hotter and his fingertips prickled with stray urges. Probably the urge to rip off that expensive gold dress and sink into the soft flesh beneath.

He hurled a curse. How could he think such a thing about his brother's wife? He hadn't wanted to come back here, and this was a perfect example of why. He lived a nice, sensible life in L.A.—well, by L.A. standards—where things like this just didn't happen.

Still…he'd dated more than his fair share of women and he'd never been kissed like that before. Curiosity mingled with the lust thickening in his blood. There was clearly a lot more to Lani Rahia than he'd expected.

That night, AJ sat three seats away from Lani at an official state banquet observing his brother's passing. Dressed in mourning blue, with an elaborate gold necklace that probably weighed more than she did, she looked every bit the royal widow.

Ears pricked, he listened for her voice. She barely spoke, though, only offering polite morsels of conversation when necessary. When he glanced her way, her lips were pressed together, as if trying to keep something in—or perhaps, after this afternoon, to keep something out.

He attempted to hold up his end of the conversation with an elderly member of the royal guard who shamelessly checked international cricket scores on his phone in between courses. By the time dessert was served, AJ had resolved to corner Lani and ask her what happened this afternoon.

His plan was thwarted when Lani vanished halfway through the fish course. There was some commotion, and a footman went to help her to her room.

He turned to his mother, seated diagonally across the table. "What's going on? Where's Lani gone?"

She patted her lips with a napkin. "Not feeling well. Poor Lani's taken Vanu's death so badly. She's been in and out of bed since he disappeared." She reached over and patted his arm. "I'm glad you care. She's a sweet girl."

AJ cleared his throat. "I'm sure she is."

"Perhaps you could go look in on her after dinner." A thoughtful smile crossed her lips. "Just to see if she's comfortable."

"I'll do that." Had grief caused her unexpected response earlier? He shuddered with revulsion at the sudden idea that she'd mistake him for his dead brother. Did her disappearance from dinner have anything to do with their unexpectedly passionate kiss?

Either way, he wanted to know more.

Lani slammed her bedroom door closed and leaned against it. Alone. It wasn't easy to get even one minute by yourself in a royal palace. Nausea rose inside her like a wave, and she planted her feet on the floor to ride it out. Was it guilt that drove this sickness to surge and torment her day and night?

Or something else?

She listened for footsteps. No sound except the evening song of insects in the gardens outside. Now was the perfect time. Everyone in the palace was either eating at the banquet, or waiting on the diners. Even her mother-in-law, who hovered over her day and night, wouldn't leave her guests until the meal was done.

Lani crept across the room and switched on the light in the adjoining bathroom. It gleamed with the rich gold-veined marble and the solid-gold taps Vanu had installed. He'd loved to luxuriate in the bath while she massaged the knotted sinews of his arms and back. It was still hard to believe he'd never glare at her from across the room and hurl an unreasonable demand again.

Guilt snaked through her. She shouldn't think

such thoughts about the dead. It was bad luck, if nothing else.

She crept into the small private changing room where she kept her personal items. Buried among the tampons she knew no one would disturb was a prize she'd gone to great lengths to obtain.

She held her breath as she fished inside the box and felt for the packet. Her fingers stung with fear as they rested on its plastic cover. She glanced over her shoulder before she pulled it out, then she ripped open the packet and reached for the printed instructions inside.

Another wave of nausea blurred her eyes and made her clutch at the nearby wall, fingernails scraping on the hard, carved stone. Then she drew a deep breath. Better get it over with.

Hold stick in stream of urine. Place on level surface for thirty seconds. Plus sign indicates a positive result. Minus sign indicates a negative result, she read from the package.

Stomach clenched and hands shaking, she followed the instructions, then paced the large bathroom while she waited for the results. How odd that she'd wanted a child so much when they first married. Dreamed of holding her son or daughter in her arms and lavishing him or her with kisses and smiles.

Then when Vanu had revealed himself to be heartless, soulless, she'd prayed to remain empty so no child would have to grow up with a father like him.

It was easy; Vanu rarely touched her. If anything, he seemed repulsed by her body, by her very femininity. They hadn't been intimate for at least two years until that last night, when she'd told him exactly what she thought of him, and he'd taken her by force.

Tears sprang to her eyes and she swiped at them

with the back of her hand. The pink stick must have revealed its answer by now, but she didn't dare look. If the result was negative, then she'd done her duty as a royal wife and could maybe even slide back into the realm of ordinary people. If not, she could be the mother of a future king, a duty that would bind her for the rest of her life.

At first it hadn't occurred to her that she could be pregnant. Vanu had taken to berating her for her infertility and inability to produce an heir. He took pleasure in taunting her with this, even when conception was technically impossible because they never had sex. She'd almost started to believe his lies.

When he went missing she suffered bouts of sickness. At first she'd assumed them to be guilt-related. If she hadn't confronted him, he wouldn't have stalked off into the night. She'd told no one she was responsible for his disappearance.

As the weeks went on, her illness had been accompanied by other disturbing symptoms—moodiness, sensitive nipples and a slight thickening at her waist. No one else had noticed, but she could no longer pass these things off as "guilt" and she knew for sure they weren't from grief, as others might have suspected.

She grabbed the stick and pulled it close, willing herself to be strong. A tiny pink cross filled the circle on the handle.

She was pregnant—with Vanu's child.

She sank against the wall, breath coming in shallow gasps. What now?

A loud knock on the door made her jump. She shoved the stick into a pile of towels and rubbed the tear tracks from her eyes. "Who is it?"

"AJ." His gruff voice penetrated the heavy wood.

"I'm, er, unwell."

"I know. That's why I came."

"Thanks, but I'll be fine."

"Let me in. Please. Just for a moment."

Lani hesitated. AJ might be a hard-partying Hollywood director, but he was also next in line to the Rahiian throne. She couldn't ignore him.

She glanced in the mirror and attempted to compose the stricken face that greeted her. She slapped her cheeks to bring back some color, tucked a strand of loose hair behind her ear then hurried to the door.

AJ tapped his foot on the polished stone tile outside the door. Lani probably didn't want visitors if she wasn't feeling well, especially him. Bad enough that he was supposedly her unwilling future husband, but the events of earlier made the situation even more awkward. If she'd slapped his face and told him to get lost, everything would be going smoothly, but now...

Still, he needed to see her or he'd never sleep tonight.

The door creaked open, revealing a tiny sliver of Lani's famously beautiful face.

"Have you been crying?" The question burst from his lips. She shook her head, lips pressed together. "You're allowed to, you know. You are recently widowed."

"I know." Already fresh tears sprang up behind her dark lashes. "Sorry, it's just been such a busy week with all the ceremonies."

"You must be exhausted." Though that didn't explain the kiss. "I came to apologize for kissing you out of the blue like that." He straightened his shoulders. Funny, he hadn't come here to apologize, but the sight of her lovely face stained with tears had an uncomfortable effect on him. Even now, she was breathtaking, her long, golden brown hair streaming behind her shoulders and her lips soft and pink.

He cursed his physical reaction. Was this any way to behave with a grieving widow, even if you were supposed to marry her?

"I appreciate the apology." She almost whispered it. "I know that technically you have nothing to apologize for, since I'm supposed to marry you, but it took me by surprise."

"Took me by surprise, too." A smile tried to spread across his lips but he fought it back. "I wasn't expecting such an enthusiastic response."

Her cheeks flushed. "I don't know what happened. I've been through a lot lately. Too many emotions..." She trailed off, dropping her lashes to cover her eyes.

"And there I was taking it personally." He reached out and touched her arm, which wasn't easy since the door was barely open a foot. "Listen, no hard feelings. I meant what I said about leaving, so you don't have to worry about me trying to jump into Vanu's bed. I think I actually wanted to get you angry at me. I regret that."

"No hard feelings."

"You really are a sweet Rahiian maiden."

"Sometimes I wonder." She glanced up at him, and for a second he thought he saw a twinkle of mischief in her eye. Desire snapped through him and he fought a sudden urge to lean in and kiss her again.

"Are you sick?" He struggled to remember the reason he'd supposedly come here. Maybe he'd unwittingly hoped for another intoxicating kiss.

"Not really." An odd expression flashed across her

features—panic, almost. She glanced over his shoulder, as if expecting something frightening in the corridor. "I'll be fine. I should get some sleep." She grasped the door with her fingers, ready to close it.

"Would you like something from the kitchens?" He wasn't ready to leave yet.

She shook her head. "I'm not hungry. I ate most of the meal."

"A glass of wine, or something to help you unwind?"

Her eyes widened. "No, thanks."

"Do you want to talk? I know it's rough sometimes being a member of the royal family. You have to be on your best behavior all the time and can't let your hair down." He glanced at her impressive tresses. "And you have a lot of hair."

For a second she looked like she might smile—or even invite him in—then she glanced over his shoulder again.

This time he turned around to see if there really was anything to look at. Nothing but stars winking through the carved openings in the corridor wall.

"There's no one here. We're alone, though I'm not sure how much comfort that is to you." He smiled, trying to be reassuring. He had a weird feeling that she did want to say something.

Her lips twitched in an agonizingly sensual motion, and she blinked rapidly. "It was nice of you to come check on me. I'll be fine." Her tears had dried and her eyes shone again. Sad, but beautiful. "It's been a long day." She tilted her head slightly and looked at him though her lashes. "And I apologize for my role in the kiss. I don't know what came over me."

"No apology needed. And whatever came over

you, it was rather lovely." He flashed a smile, then an odd feeling swept through him. Another powerful urge to kiss her. Her skin looked so soft, shining in the lamplight, and he could smell her soft scent in the narrow space of the doorway. Her dark gaze seemed to call to him: Help me.

His lips met hers, hard and fast, but this time she pulled back and slammed the door. The wood bumped his forehead and sent him staggering back into the corridor, lips still buzzing from that lightning fast but incredibly powerful touch.

"Idiot." He said the word aloud and smacked his head. What was he thinking? Still, did she have to slam the door like that?

He glanced around, relieved the corridor was still empty. What was it about this woman that made him act so crazy?

Lani ran back into the bathroom, where she closed and locked the door. It had been the one safe place where she could hide from Vanu—discounting the many hours they spent safely in public spaces—where she could lock the door and shut out his cruelty.

How odd—how awful—to now be hiding from his brother.

Or was she?

Her belly tingled with stray sensation—awareness of the swift touch of his fingers as he leaned in to kiss her. His lips had brushed hers for a split second, but seemed to have branded her with fire. If she hadn't slammed the door so fast she'd have rushed into his arms.

Which meant that yes, she was hiding from him.

And she was hiding from her mother-in-law. She'd

have to tell her about the pregnancy immediately, before it became any more obvious.

Just now she'd fought a strange, almost insane urge to tell AJ everything when he asked her if she wanted to talk. What wouldn't she give to be able to confide in someone? To seek comfort in a pair of strong arms that wanted to soothe and comfort her rather than to hurt her.

Lani shivered. She'd been through so much in the past few years. Even though Vanu had rarely touched her, his tongue could bite hard as a lash. His brother was so different. Famous as a playboy, AJ seemed laid-back and warm, easy going and nonjudgmental. What would it be like to have a relationship with someone who genuinely liked people?

Not that she'd ever find out. Of course he wouldn't stay. He had a life—a big, famous life—to get back to. Rahiri was a little speck of forested land in the middle of the wide Pacific to him. It wasn't his home anymore.

For a split second she envied him his freedom. It must take some confidence to walk away from the royal family he'd been born into.

For the last few weeks she'd entertained thoughts of having a normal life, maybe even going back to New Jersey to visit her father and her two stepsisters who were now in high school. It would be fun to just, say, go to a mall and giggle over some shoes.

A long sigh slid from her mouth. After tonight's news, that would never happen.

She reached down and pulled the stick out of its hiding place amongst the fresh towels. Yes, the little pink cross was still there, sealing her fate as the mother of the newest member of the royal Rahiian dynasty.

* * *

The next morning, after an almost completely sleepless night, Lani approached her mother-in-law at breakfast and asked if they could meet privately.

"Lani, you look terrible!" Priia Rahia took her daughter-in-law's face in her hands. "We all loved Vanu, but you must take care of yourself. Eat some eggs, and some papaya." She loaded the ripe fruit onto Lani's plate. "And of course I'll talk to you." She gave a bright smile.

Much as Lani loved her mother-in-law, she could often hear the wheels turning behind Priia's composed expression. She probably imagined this would be a private chat about her future relationship with AJ—a million miles away from her intended purpose.

Maybe something in her expression made Priia realize the situation was serious. "Come with me right now. Bring your breakfast and eat in my study."

The older woman hooked her arm through Lani's and guided her out past the stone-faced waiters. "Bring fresh tea," she called behind her.

Marching down the hallway, her mother-in-law looked crisp and efficient as always, her black hair short and glossy, her traditional dress perfectly arranged over her neat, plump body. She projected an aura of calm and warmth that Lani had appreciated so much over the last few years, though that had been shaken by Vanu's disappearance and presumed death.

Lani was shivering slightly by the time they reached the shell-pink sanctuary on the east side of the house. Morning sun streamed through the windows, illuminating her mother-in-law's collection of bird statues and the traditional embroideries she made into cushions and wall hangings.

"Take a seat." Priia pointed to a plush pink armchair. "Be sure to eat. You've looked pale lately. Are you feeling better?"

She swallowed. "A little." She looked down at her plate; the contents looked inedible. "I'm not really sick." Her heart started to pound. "I've just been feeling ill because…"

Priia tilted her head, expectant. Her lips pursed into a familiar smile. "What, dear?"

"I'm pregnant." The words fell out on a sigh.

Priia's eyes snapped open. "Did I hear you right? You're expecting?"

Lani nodded, unable to push words past the lump in her throat. "I think so." No need to mention that she'd taken a test. She had all the usual symptoms, anyway. "At first I thought it was stress over Vanu's disappearance, but now I'm pretty sure it's…" She glanced down at her stomach, which appeared flat beneath the green and blue pattern of her dress.

"A baby." Priia clapped her hands together and a broad smile lit her face. "How marvelous!"

"Yes," whispered Lani.

"A ray of light in our darkest hour." Priia sprang to her feet and strode across the room. "A miracle."

It didn't really feel that way to Lani, which only added to her crippling burden of guilt. She should be happy. A baby was always a reason to celebrate in Rahiri.

Unless it was the child of your unloved and evil late husband.

"We must celebrate. We'll plan a big party. What a marvelous way to move forward after the sad days of the funeral." Priia was almost dancing around the room.

"A baby! Our Vanu's child will carry on his legacy here in the palace."

Lani bit her lip. That's what she was worried about. Which wasn't fair. The innocent child might be nothing like Vanu at all. Everyone else in the royal family was warm and kind, including the father-in-law who'd died before she came.

"Oh, sweet little baby clothes. I must start embroidering right away." Priia patted Lani's cheek affectionately. "I wonder if he will have your lovely golden coloring. Or it could be a she." She frowned. "Of course we won't know for—" She grasped Lani's arms. "How far along are you?"

"I'm not really sure." She didn't want to pinpoint the night Vanu disappeared, though that was certainly the date of conception. "A few weeks, at least. I'm just starting to show."

"Oh, do let me look at you." Priia snatched Lani's untouched plate from her lap and tugged her to her feet. She patted the rumpled fabric over her belly. "I can't feel much yet, but I took a while to show with my boys. We Rahias don't have large babies, but they grow up to be big strong men." Her beaming grin was almost infectious.

Almost. Lani struggled to look at least slightly happy about the circumstance, but instead her lip wanted to tremble.

"You're worried, aren't you? Scared." Priia took Lani in her soft arms. Her expensive scent enveloped her for a moment. "I know it's not easy having a baby when you're a widow. The child reminds you of the man you've lost."

Lani looked down. Her words were painfully true.

"But look on it as a wonderful chance to let him live again through his child."

Please, no! Lani blinked rapidly, trying to keep her emotions in check.

Priia pressed a finger to her lips. "Though this does rather complicate things with AJ. It's not easy for a man to raise another man's child, even if it is his brother's."

"I don't think AJ wants to marry me." Lani said the words quickly.

"Don't take it personally. He's just gotten off track with this Hollywood business. He'll realize that his duty lies with us in Rahiri." Her mother-in-law's face grew serious. "Oh, my goodness."

"What?" Lani's chest grew tight at the look of alarm in Priia's dark eyes.

"According to our laws of succession, the baby is next in line to the throne." She stared at Lani, her face growing pale.

Thoughts clicked into place. "So AJ doesn't inherit the throne."

"Not if Vanu has a child." Priia bustled across the room and stared out the window toward the forest. Then she spun around. "Oh, I do so want AJ back home with us. He was so unsettled as a child, always jealous of Vanu and in a rush to get away. I'm sure things would be different now that he's grown and matured. Now that my husband and oldest son are gone, it would warm my heart to have my youngest son here with us. And I do believe he'd be a very good husband to you."

Lani remained silent. A stray memory of his lips on hers assaulted her and caused color to rise to her cheeks. She had no idea what kind of husband AJ would be, and she'd rather not find out—kiss or no kiss. Vanu was enough husband for one lifetime.

Priia's expression hardened. "Don't say anything. Don't mention the baby."

"To AJ?"

"To anyone." She gripped Lani's wrists. "Let no one find out until you're safely married to AJ. Then they can think it's his."

Revulsion at the proposed deception coiled in Lani's already queasy gut. "But I'm weeks along, almost two months."

Priia loosened her grip and rubbed Lani's arm—which didn't feel all that soothing over the goose bumps that had formed there. "You can say it's premature. We really do have small babies. Even big, strapping AJ was barely six pounds at birth. No one will ever find out."

"You wouldn't even tell AJ?"

"Why? Better to let him think the baby is his." She tilted her head and looked right into Lani's eyes. "Sometimes men are happier if we keep some secrets from them. It's part of our work as women to keep the world running smoothly."

Lani could feel a cold sweat breaking out on her back. "I don't like deception. And what if AJ doesn't want to marry me?"

Priia's lips formed a tight smile. "He will."

Three

AJ's plane left for L.A. at six o'clock the following morning. He was not on it.

"Thank you, sweetheart." His mom's expression alternated between tears and smiles. "You don't know how much it means to me to have you here. I couldn't survive the loss of one son if I didn't have another."

AJ didn't really follow her logic—or like it one bit—but he nodded. Apparently he had no resistance to female pleading and weeping. Hopefully in a few days his mom would calm down and he could make his escape.

"Have some papaya, sweetheart." She pushed a platter laden with the shiny golden fruit toward him.

His stomach recoiled. "I'm not hungry." The bright sunlight flooding the breakfast room contrasted strongly with his mood. Lani picked at her own breakfast on the other side of the big, polished table. He kept his eyes firmly off her. She had a very unsettling effect on him, and he didn't need any more crazy things happening. Getting a door slammed in his kisser was quite enough.

His mom clapped her hands together, bracelets jangling. "We're going to plan a party."

Lani's head shot up. He sneaked a glance at her, and saw her eyes wide with alarm.

"Isn't this an odd time for a party?" AJ leaned back in his chair. "Especially after all the funeral events. Lani's probably exhausted."

Lani didn't meet his gaze, just stared at her teacup.

"I think it's important to show people that this is not an end for the Rahias, it's a new beginning." His mom's crisp smile had firmly replaced her tears.

A sense of foreboding hummed in AJ's gut. He strongly suspected that he played a key role in that "new beginning." "I really can't stay long, Mom. I have script meetings for my new movie."

"You could do them via teleconferencing. We have it set up in the throne room."

"It's not the same." He didn't want to go anywhere near the blasted throne room. There really was a throne in there—an impossibly ancient piece of volcanic rock carved with mysterious markings—and he had a nasty feeling he'd end up on top of it if he wasn't careful.

"Of course it is. And Lani and I can be your assistants, can't we dear?" She shone her megawatt smile on Lani.

Who gulped, visibly. "Oh yes. I do enjoy your films." Her voice was as flat as her expression.

"What do you like better, the violence or the sex?"

"There isn't really that much of either." She tilted her elegant head and her long mane of brown hair swung in front of one shoulder. "What makes your movies so good is that you use suspense and anticipation to keep the audience on their toes. Teenage boys probably think they saw all that stuff when they leave the theater, but really you kept their hearts pounding by making them think it was going to happen, or had just happened. It's very clever."

AJ's mouth hung open for a second. "You really have watched them."

"That's why we installed the theater, dear." His mother patted her lips with a napkin.

Lani's eyes sparkled. She was clearly delighted to defy his expectations. Her bright gaze sent a shimmer of—something straight to his core.

Great. Just what he needed.

"We're your biggest fans." His mother patted his hand. "And we'll have the party this Saturday."

"How can you plan it so quickly?"

She smiled. "Easy, dear. No one turns down an invitation to the palace, and we have the most talented and creative staff in the Pacific."

"There is that." AJ winked at her. "You really are something, Mom. If a party will make you feel better, you go ahead and have one."

"You will be there."

"I'll be there." He didn't hide the sigh of resignation in his voice. How could you argue with your own grieving mother? "Just don't ask me to make any speeches."

"Why don't you two go pick some flowers? We'll use them to decorate the ballroom."

AJ raised an eyebrow. A flower-picking expedition? Clearly his mom had not given up on the idea of getting them together. "I'm sure the flowers are happier in the ground."

"Nonsense. They bloom better if you pluck them from time to time. Don't they, Lani?"

Lani smiled. "Some of them do. I'll go get the shears and some jugs for them." She didn't look at AJ.

His mom's lips curved into a smile. "Take good care of Lani, won't you? Don't let her strain herself."

AJ glanced at Lani, who once again was looking away. No doubt she was quite capable of deciding just how much strain she could handle. His mom probably had visions of him carrying her up hills or lifting her delicately over puddles. Hopefully Lani wouldn't expect him to, as he had no intention of going within five feet of her. She was dangerous.

They set off into the gardens, AJ carrying two metal jugs. Lani tucked a pair of shears into the pocket of her dress. It had rained overnight—as it usually did—and the leaves glistened with raindrops. A swallow darted around them as they headed toward the orchid forest down a narrow path of carved stones. Lani had removed her sandals and walked barefoot, Rahiian style. AJ kept his Skechers on, though he regretted it as they became increasingly sodden. "I'd forgotten how wet it is here."

"That's why they call it the rainforest." Lani shot him a cheeky look. The unusual golden color of her eyes struck him and he snatched his gaze away.

"Soggy, is what I call it. Now, L.A. has my kind of climate. A nice dry desert."

"With a decorative haze of smog." Lani marched straight ahead, her pretty toes splayed on the mossy stones.

"Exactly. Who needs to see all those mountains anyway? Hey, there's a flower." A delicate bloom peeked its head around the trunk of a tree.

"Lovely." Lani stopped and walked up to it. "But it's rather a rare orchid that only blooms every four years. I think we should leave it to enjoy its moment of glory here in this beautiful place. I'm not sure it would be happy in the ballroom."

AJ snorted. "I'm not sure anyone's ever happy in that ballroom, but they darn sure pretend to be. Why is Mom so good at getting what she wants?"

"She puts a lot of energy into everything she does. And she's a very loving person."

"Yes, she loves it when things go her way."

"She's always treated me like a daughter."

"You are her daughter. In law, at least."

"My mom runs a laundry and my dad is American. I'm hardly Rahiian aristocracy. She could have treated me quite differently."

AJ shrugged. "So? Snobbery is not really a Rahiian thing. You're probably more aware of it because of your years in America. Was it odd moving here from New Jersey? It must have been quite the lifestyle change."

She laughed. "I missed my bike. And my friend Kathy. I loved the beaches and all the colorful birds." She tucked a strand of hair behind her ears. "And of course I missed my dad."

"They got divorced?"

"Yup. My mom never really became Americanized. She refused to learn to drive, and she hated being out in crowded shops, so she tended to buy everything at the corner store."

"If corner stores in New Jersey are anything like the ones in L.A., she was getting ripped off."

"I'm sure. She didn't like American clothes and

wouldn't cut her hair. At first my dad thought all those things were cute, but after a few years he got tired of her traditional attitudes and began pushing her to adapt."

"But she didn't."

"She couldn't. She's very shy. She probably only married him in the first place because she was too timid to say no." Lani bent down to smell a pretty white lily at the base of a tree.

"Or he swept her off her feet."

"Probably some of that, too." She walked ahead, veering from the path into a little tunnel through the undergrowth. "But after eight years he called it quits and packed her off back home."

AJ ducked to avoid wet leaves brushing his hair. "Did Vanu sweep you off your feet?"

She flinched slightly, just a slight tic of her shoulders.

"It must be painful to think about him."

"It's okay. It wasn't really like that. Vanu saw me in the marketplace one day. He liked the look of me, and your mom found out who I was and invited me to the palace. It was all very formal. The marriage proposal was delivered to our house—behind the laundry, of course—by his footman."

"Not very romantic." AJ watched her slender form, clad in its delicate floral pattern, stepping daintily through the forest.

"Not at all. I didn't even know him at that point. We'd had about five minutes of conversation."

"So why did you agree to marry him?"

She shrugged. "Everyone said I had to. There really wasn't any question of not marrying him. My mom would never have forgiven me, for one thing, so I'd have spent the rest of my life in the laundry with her glaring at me." She made a face.

"I see what you mean. Well, rest assured this time. Even my mom can't force you and I to get married."

She froze, then kept walking. For a second she wrapped her arms around herself like she was cold—impossible since it was already at least eighty-five degrees, even in the lush shade.

"Have I offended you?" He snatched a leaf from a nearby shrub, then wondered why he'd done it. He pressed the plump, succulent leaf between his fingers.

"Not at all. I admire your independent attitude."

"You could always develop one yourself, you know." He was tempted to reach out and prod her in the ribs, but pulled his hand back at the last second. Even the thought of touching her made his fingertips prickle with awareness.

She was silent for a moment. "No. I couldn't let your mother down. She's been too good to me. She's lonely, you know, since your father died. She misses him very much. And now, losing Vanu…" She rubbed her arm, as if soothing goose bumps.

"She's lucky to have you, Lani."

"She's expecting us to find some flowers. We'd better get to work." Her wry glance made heat flash in his core. Didn't mean anything really. She was stunning—anyone would be attracted to her. Seductive, almond-shaped eyes fringed with dark lashes, her perfect small nose, her finely cut, sensual mouth…then all that sleek, golden brown hair falling about her slim shoulders. If she weren't his sister-in-law he'd want to put her in a movie.

"I guess we'd better find some it's okay to cut. You lead the way."

He followed her across a wide lawn surrounded by yellow hibiscus in full bloom, then down a little hill toward the nearby beach. He could smell the ocean in the air, crisp and salty and slightly fishy.

"These are my favorites." She pointed to white petunias, scattered like confetti at their feet where the jungle faded into the beach.

AJ glanced at the Rahiian ocean for the first time in years. Bright turquoise, it stretched forever, the horizon punctuated only by the nearby island of Naluua—an emerald dot fringed with white, floating in the clear blue bowl of sea and sky. "Damn."

Lani glanced up. "What?"

"I forgot the power of the sea."

Humor sparkled in her golden eyes. "They say the ocean in California is stunning."

"Not like this." He kicked off his shoes and strode out onto the fine white sand. The silky texture wrapped around his toes like a familiar embrace. "And ours is always warm." The beach wasn't wide. He reached the water in less than twenty strides, then stood while a small wave swept in sea foam to cover his toes. "Ahhh, now that feels good."

Lani laughed. A sweet, high, golden sound. It echoed and thrilled somewhere deep in his chest. He glanced at her, and basked in the warmth of her smile. It felt good to see her look happy, even if only for a moment. "Come on in." He extended his hand.

He regretted the gesture instantly. Touching her was definitely a bad idea. His skin tingled and the hairs on his arm stood on end even at the prospect.

It was likely she felt the same way, as she walked gingerly across the sand and dipped her toes into the water a good ten feet away. She sighed as the water swept around her delicate ankles. "I haven't done this in a long time. You take the water for granted when you live here."

"I guess you have to be gone a while to appreciate it." The sun warmed his face while the water lapped over his toes and his heels sank deeper into the soft sand. "Vanu and I used to spend hours down here, hunting for different shells and insects. It certainly is a good place for a kid to grow up."

Lani's smile vanished. AJ frowned. He shouldn't have mentioned Vanu. She obviously missed him. Maybe her Vanu was very different from the one he remembered? Brothers often had adversarial relationships.

He tried to ignore the recoil in his gut as he thought of her in Vanu's arms. Which was insane, since she was Vanu's wife. And how could he feel jealous over a woman he didn't have or even want?

The wind whipped Lani's hair to one side, revealing her striking profile. Okay, maybe he did want her. But not in any way that was appropriate under the circumstances. She wasn't some bubbly production assistant looking for a spot on the casting couch, or a cheeky starlet hoping for a bit part as well as some action.

Maybe that was part of the appeal. At least with Lani he knew she had absolutely no interest in scoring a part in one of his movies. Lately he'd found himself suspecting even the most seemingly sensible women of having ulterior motives for dating him. That's just how it was in L.A. Everyone seemed to have an agenda.

Then again, maybe Lani had an agenda, too, but he hadn't sniffed it out yet.

* * *

Lani snuck a sideways look at AJ. Proud head tilted to the horizon, he looked every bit like one of the ancient Rahiian carvings of The Old Ones. Which was funny, because until now, she'd have described him as a classic Hollywood bad boy. With his slicked-back dark hair, mischievous grin and wide, highly kissable mouth, he must have women chasing him through Beverly Hills. But now, in the strong light of the sun reflected off the ocean, she could see nothing but the classic planes of his face and the powerful body of an ancient warrior-god.

She blew out a breath. Was this really a useful line of thought?

Perhaps it was, since Priia was counting on her to convince AJ to marry her. She might as well find him attractive in that case. Guilt rippled over her like the seawater at her feet. She was supposed to trick him into marrying her so she could pass off her baby as his. Could she even live with herself if she did that?

She remembered his comment about this being a good place for a kid to grow up. She tried to imagine Vanu as a child, but couldn't. The innocence and curiosity of childhood seemed totally at odds with Vanu's harsh cynicism.

"Why did you leave Rahiri?" The question was blunt, but she wanted to know.

AJ looked out at the horizon, frowning. "Too small for me."

"You wanted to live somewhere with more going on?" She dug her toes into the sand. If he did somehow get suckered into marrying her, he'd be bored within a week.

"Yes. And where I could figure out what I really

wanted to do. Here my whole life was mapped out already—brother to the future king. I wanted more."

"And you found it." His life in L.A. must be exciting, fun. Rahiri was pleasant, but it was a peaceful place. No doubt he found it dull.

"I did." He turned to her, his expression oddly determined. "I went to college, discovered film and the rest is history." A wry grin lifted one corner of his mouth. "Okay, not exactly history, but cult film history, anyway. I enjoy my life."

How could his mom expect him to give up the life he loved and move back here, where once again his life would be mapped out for him? Cold fear mingled with the guilt trickling through her. She didn't want to be a party to spoiling AJ's life.

"Was it hard to leave?"

"Not at all." He turned a frank expression to her. "Vanu was the future king, and I was just the younger brother. I was a bit of a hell-raiser in my teens, too. I think everyone heaved a sigh of relief when I got on that plane to L.A."

"I know your mom missed you."

"And I missed her, but that doesn't mean it would have been better for me to stay here. Aren't we supposed to be finding flowers for her?"

"Yes." Lani glanced back at the green growth at the edge of the beach. "We're not doing a very good job. Honestly, I hate picking flowers. They look so much prettier and happier attached to their roots."

"Then we won't pick any. Let me guess, you think I'd be happier back here attached to my roots." Lani froze. He asked the question casually, looking up the beach and even walking away from her. He wasn't putting her on the spot.

Should she say the things her mother-in-law would want? That he'd be happy and content in the bosom of his family and helping the people of Rahiri?

She couldn't. "I don't know. If you love the life you have, it seems a shame to give it up."

The soft lapping of the ocean softened the silence between them. He slowed and she caught up with him. Tension stiffened his broad shoulders, pulling them tight against his collarless pale cotton shirt.

She watched him closely. "Do you feel a sense of duty to Rahiri?"

That question was fair enough. The son of a king was born to a life of duty, even a younger son. It did no harm to remind him of that.

He turned to face her, brows lowered. "I didn't, before. I was glad to leave all that to Vanu. There wasn't room for two of us here. Now that he's gone..." He turned to stare along the beach, where it rounded the corner of the cove and disappeared behind a clump of palm trees. "I don't know. Maybe I do feel a few stirrings of something. It's a shame you and Vanu didn't have a child, then there'd be another heir and I'd be off the hook."

Lani swallowed. She was glad he wasn't looking at her, as her face involuntarily tightened. If she told him about the baby... She fought to stop her hand rising to her stomach.

The baby. Again, guilt cascaded through her. She'd hardly given a thought to the new life growing inside her. Terror and misgivings far outweighed any joy she should feel as a new mother.

She'd wanted a baby so badly, but that was before she understood how complicated, difficult and painful life could be, even when on the surface everything was smooth and appeared normal. Vanu had awakened her to a sinister undercurrent that could spoil even the happiest of circumstances.

Although he was gone, she could still feel its dark tides tugging at her, enveloping her in this mess of subterfuge and obligation that threatened to trap AJ into an unwanted marriage.

She did feel a sense of duty, though. There was no denying the obligation—the love—she felt for her mother-in-law. If only there was a solution that would make everyone happy.

A thought occurred to her. "The country needs an heir." Her voice was low, soft, almost lost in the sound of the ocean and the rustling of leaves. "You could come back and rule…without marrying me."

AJ turned to her. At first he was frowning, then his brow softened and he looked like he might smile. "I could take that personally."

"I just want you to know that the two things don't have to be linked."

"According to tradition, they do."

"Traditions can be updated. It's the twenty-first century." And perhaps the laws of succession could be adjusted to make AJ and his heirs successors, instead of her unborn baby.

She was grasping at straws and she knew it.

AJ glanced down at her hand, which had come to rest on her belly. She pulled it away like it burned. He looked at her curiously for a second, then turned and walked back up the beach, still carrying the two empty brass jugs. "Ninety days until the successor must be chosen." His words carried on the breeze. "I haven't counted but we can't be too far off."

Lani's stomach clenched. "It's been fifty-two days

so far. Your mom is keeping count on an abacus." This also meant she was fifty-two days into her pregnancy—soon she'd really start to show.

AJ shoved a hand through his hair. "I don't know why, but I never thought I'd be in this position." He turned to face her, squinting against the bright sun. "I'd left Rahiri behind, a collection of memories and familiar faces that I'd visit from time to time but never actually return to." He blew out hard. "I don't fit here anymore."

Lani swallowed. "You have your own life. I understand that." Though she was certain his mother and the island elders wouldn't sympathize too readily. He was in a tough spot. At least she had the good luck of having absolutely no choice whatsoever. Her fate was tied to the royal dynasty, no matter what. "Only you can decide what to do."

"How can I simply decide to marry my brother's wife?" He finally put the two jugs—still empty—down in the sand and strode toward her. He picked up her hands and held them. "How can I take a woman I've barely met, and pledge my life to her?" He looked down at her hands, tiny in his. Already heat snapped between them in the warm morning air. AJ stiffened, perhaps also feeling the unsettling power. "I don't know you."

"Does anyone ever really know anyone else?" The cryptic reply rose to her lips. Her body shivered slightly. The proximity to his powerful chest seemed to stir something inside her.

"Perhaps not. We're all works in progress, after all. Maybe lives can be cast, like a film, and then we take up our roles and see what we can make of them." His dark eyes fixed on hers in a penetrating stare. "Do you think so, Lani?"

There was an edge to his voice that tightened the tension snapping through her. "Some would say you were cast in the role of royal son the day you were born." That answer would be approved by her mother-in-law.

She wanted so badly not to say the wrong thing, to ruin everything for the family and for Rahiri. If it was her fate to marry a strange man who didn't want her, then so be it. She could put up with almost anything after her years with Vanu. At least AJ seemed warm and kind.

And he was very handsome. Sun shone on the stern planes of his face as he looked down at her, confusion roiling in his narrowed eyes. His hands still held hers, tight, and heat was building between their entwined fingertips.

Lani tried to root herself firmly in the soft sand, to stay grounded no matter what might happen. Would he try to kiss her again? This time she must accept the kiss. That's what everyone would want. Her lips pulsed in anticipation and heat bloomed deep in her belly.

AJ's mouth, however, was set in a hard line, his brow furrowed. He dropped her hands and pulled back, then wiped his palms on his khaki pants. Lani's arms fell to her sides, fingertips prickling at their sudden abandonment.

Relief trickled through her, along with the ever-present guilt and a thickening fear of what the future held for all of them.

"You know what? I think we should pick some flowers for the party," AJ said gruffly. "At least we can manage not to disappoint my mom on that score."

"Of course." She tried to sound crisp and sensible. "I know a grove where we can fill both jugs without damaging the growing plants. Follow me." She marched past him up the sand, then wondered if it was appropriate to command a royal son—a future king, perhaps—to follow her. Life was so confusing once you became entangled with centuries of tradition and expectation. A foolish girl, she'd had no idea what she was getting into. What she was getting her future children into.

She heard AJ's steady footfalls behind her. He was too confident, too at home with himself to get upset by following a woman. What a refreshing change from Vanu, who would have spent the whole day needling her with the error of her ways. And AJ's solid presence behind her was reassuring. Since Vanu disappeared she'd become afraid of being alone out here in the jungle. What if he suddenly reappeared, crueler than ever, to take his revenge on her for being happy that he'd vanished?

What would AJ think about that? That she was happy his brother was dead. Yet another secret she had to carry with her to the grave. The burden made her heavy on her feet.

Her hand had strayed to her belly again and she jerked it away. "Not much farther." If only she could tell him about the baby. If he knew all the facts, they could really talk, and come to some decisions together. But it was her duty—her royal obligation—to remain silent.

They reached a shady grove where lush white lilies clustered around the trunks of trees. "We can cut these. They only bloom for a few days, and they reproduce like crazy." She pulled the small shears from her pocket and cut a clump of stems. The full, pale blooms looked suddenly bereft, severed from their roots. She shoved them quickly into AJ's offered jug.

"Lucky flowers to live such a carefree existence. And now they get to attend one of Mom's royal balls." His warm grin evaporated some of the gloom that had settled over her. "At least the party will keep her busy for a few days so she won't be too sad."

"She does love organizing things." Lani smiled. "And she's never happier than when surrounded by a thousand of her closest friends."

"And I guess you and I can plaster smiles on our faces for an evening. Though you can imagine what they'll all be thinking."

Lani bit her lip. "Yes. I think I can."

"They'll be whispering—so, is that film-director son going to marry the widow?" He spoke in a funny, Rahiian busybody voice that made Lani laugh, despite the ball of dread that had settled firmly at the bottom of her stomach.

"They will. Most likely they'll assume it, since you're still here."

"We could walk around scowling at each other, just to make things exciting and keep them guessing." He shot her a wry smile.

Lani managed to smile back. They had every reason to keep guessing. She certainly was. Would AJ agree to marry her? Would he believe her "premature baby" was really his? Or would he take off back to L.A., leaving her to raise her child by herself?

Or was there another outcome, perhaps harsher than she could even imagine, that had not yet presented itself?

Four

Violin music hummed over the murmur of a thousand conversations as the ballroom filled to capacity with Priia's invited guests. Sweat prickled inside AJ's stiff collar. He wore a starched black tunic and matching pants, a funerary version of Rahiian party attire. The sleek getup would look downright hip on the streets of Beverley Hills, but the traditional garb made him itch as if he'd stepped into someone else's skin.

"Arun!" He startled at the sound of his given name—no one ever used it—and glanced up to see a white-haired man approaching. AJ immediately recognized his father's oldest friend. Despite his stiffened gait and wrinkled visage, the old man's eyes twinkled as brightly as ever as he gripped AJ in a fierce embrace. "It's so good to see you back home again. Your return brings both tears and smiles to all our eyes."

AJ swallowed. "It's good to be back." The lie scorched his tongue and he took a quick swig of punch. "How are you these days, sir?"

"Sir? Sir!" The tanned face creased into a million lines. "What way is that for our new king to address one of his subjects. You should call me Niuu like all these other overdressed fools."

Our new king.

AJ fought the urge to come right out and say "I'm not staying," but he didn't want to ruin his mom's party. "I'll try. Old habits are hard to break. I feel a bit like a kid again, surrounded by all my parents' old friends."

"You are a kid, my boy, at least compared to me, and that's what Rahiri needs. Fresh energy to take us into the future. You will keep making films, won't you? My wife and I do enjoy the *Dragon Chaser* series."

"Films, yes, I imagine so." It was the ruling Rahiri part he didn't intend on. "I'm surprised people here watch my films."

"We're so proud of you, Arun, making a name for yourself and for our island in Hollywood."

AJ fought a smile. He certainly didn't think of himself as representing Rahiri with his work. Maybe that is how people here saw it, though. He'd never given the matter much thought.

The old man grasped his upper arm. "Do keep funding the schools, won't you? They're our future. So much young talent on this island. And our healthcare system is second to none. Your father put all that in place, and it will take a strong guiding hand to keep the rudder steady as you lead us into the future." The gnarled fingers tightened around his biceps. "You're strong, all right. Built like one of the ancient ones! Quite unlike your brother, Vanu." The man's expression grew clouded. "We're all sorry for his loss, of course, but ready to move into the future under your capable leadership."

"I appreciate your faith in me." AJ searched his brain for things to say that didn't disappoint but didn't actually commit him to anything. Or make his growing guilt any more agonizing.

"Naturally I have faith in you. You're your father's son. He raised you to be a man and take responsibility for those in need." He clapped his other hand on AJ's bicep, holding him in a kind of armlock. "We need you, Arun, and we're proud to have you as our new king."

AJ opened his mouth but no words came out. He glanced over the old man's shoulder and caught sight of Lani on the other side of the room. Standing dead still amidst the swirling crowds, she looked pale and lost. "Please excuse me."

He hurried through the crowd, managing nods and waves to faces he hadn't seen in years. Lani didn't even see him approach. Her eyes were fixed high on a carved column, her expression vacant, as if trying to forget where she was.

"Lani, you okay?"

She jumped and blinked. "Of course." Her wide eyes gave her a startled expression.

"You look like a three-toed sloth who's accidentally fallen out of her tree onto a multilane highway."

"Funny, since that exactly how I feel." A tiny smile tugged at the edges of her lovely mouth—then disappeared.

"Too many people wanting something from you? I

know how that is." What did Lani want? If he asked, he knew she'd give him the party line from his mom rather than a straight answer. She'd say she wanted to marry him, whether she did or not. And why would she? They'd barely met and weren't at all suited to each other. He was a hard-partying film director and she was a quiet village girl—albeit a royal one. "You don't look well."

"I'm fine." The words flew from her lips and she lifted her shoulders, like she was trying to convince herself as well as him. "Just a little tired. I haven't been sleeping well lately."

Probably still grieving for Vanu. Again he felt that unfamiliar prick of jealousy. Which was ridiculous. How could he begrudge his brother anything now that he was dead? This whole crazy situation was messing with his mind.

"Maybe you should go somewhere and sit down." He offered his arm, bracing himself against the powerful effect she had on him.

She didn't move. Her dark lashes lowered, then she looked up at him with those haunting golden eyes. "I'm fine, really. I'll make more of an effort from now on. Your mom needs me to. And we'll be stuck sitting down for hours once the speeches start."

"The speeches. That's one part of Rahiian culture I really haven't missed. Has anyone broken a new record for longest speech ever?"

"I think it's still at five hours." She smiled. "At least it's very relaxing for the listeners. And you know you'll have to make a speech."

He grimaced. He would, too. What on earth would he say? Usually he was good at speaking off the cuff, but the stakes were a little higher here than at an investors' meeting. "You're lucky being a girl, so you're off the hook. If I do become king I'm going to change that right away so all the ladies get to make speeches, too."

Lani's eyes widened, but they sparkled with humor. "Your mom would love that. She'd go on all night."

"Wouldn't she?" He laughed. They both knew he was joking about becoming king.

Wasn't he?

Lani watched AJ melt back into the well-dressed throng amidst smiles and exclamations. He stood almost a full head above most people in the room, and moved like a king among them with his broad shoulders and easy, confident manner. Everyone in the region was happy to see him back. Pleased that the Rahiian succession would be a smooth and effortless affair following time-honored methods.

People kept a respectful distance from her. As a widow in mourning, she was not expected to eat and dance and chatter along with the guests.

But they all expected her to marry AJ. They just had no idea he didn't want to.

She wasn't sure whether to feel relieved or alarmed. He seemed to have every intention of going back to L.A. He'd said nothing to suggest otherwise and he hadn't asked her opinion, either. If he had, of course she'd have said she wanted to marry him. What else could she say?

Her fingers had stung with anticipation just now when he reached out to give her his arm. All the tiny hairs on her arm had stood on end, craving his touch.

Now she wondered if she'd done the wrong thing in refusing.

The whole situation was so confusing and disturbing. She was expected to entice him to marry her—immediately—but she didn't want to trap him into a lifetime deception she'd be forced to maintain.

And she didn't want to be married to a man—another man—who didn't love her.

"Sweetheart, come sit down next to me. They're starting the speeches." Priia glowed with good cheer, as she always did at her festive gatherings. She bloomed and shone with the energy of other people. Naturally gregarious and effortlessly charming, she was born to be a queen. Lani envied her tireless energy and outgoing personality.

She led Lani to a cushioned chair at the high table. "Sit down." She patted the cushions. "And have some coconut stars. You need to keep your strength up."

"Thanks, you're too good to me." Lani took one of the coconut treats, then wondered what to do with it. Her stomach, hidden beneath the thick sash of her gold-embroidered dress, certainly wasn't in any condition to handle food.

"Nonsense, dear. You're the light of my old age." She leaned in, conspiratorial, eyes shining. "And soon you'll bring a new bright light to life among us."

Lani blanched and tried not to glance around. What if someone overheard and guessed what she meant?

A dignified-looking elderly man wrapped in the distinctive clothing of a nearby island walked out into the center of the floor, where the speeches took place. At first Lani sat stiffly in her seat, wondering if her fate would be pronounced or speculated upon. Instead he launched into a semi-poetic history of the region, laden with myth and superstition, and she soon let her mind drift.

Another speaker followed, then another, chanting as much as speaking, celebrating the community of the islands and the long-held peace that united them in this beautiful place. Lulled by the warm atmosphere, Lani relaxed into her cushions and even managed to nibble on her coconut star.

She sat up abruptly when the master of ceremonies called AJ—or rather Arun Jahir—to the floor. She glanced over at him, and watched him rise, face expressionless, and walk out into the center of the room. His crisp black garb emphasized the strength and dignity of his movements. Head held high and back straight, he moved like a monarch, even if he didn't want to be one.

A little flash of pride surprised Lani. She liked AJ and sympathized with the awkward situation he was in. She still didn't really understand why he'd kissed her—twice—but under the circumstances it was excusable, even if her initial response wasn't. He obviously wanted to do the right thing, but like her, he wasn't sure what that was, and he wisely knew that the wrong choice would have lasting, painful consequences.

Lani shifted in her chair, remembering the tiny consequence she carried inside her. Her fear and anxiety about the situation she found herself in now warred with stray sparks of excitement and eager anticipation of her baby's arrival. How could she not look forward to holding that tiny, warm body and feeling the grip of a plump hand on her finger?

AJ studied the crowd in silence for a few moments.

When he began to speak, his voice was deeper than she remembered. Like the others, he spoke of the long history of the royal line, the legend of how their people had first arrived on long boats from a far-off land, how they'd fought and made peace.

Lani watched, heart pounding. How did AJ manage to sound so perfectly like one of the wise men of the region? You'd never guess he'd been gone for more than a decade. He seemed to carry the cadence and rhythm of the ancient stories in his blood—his royal blood—and why wouldn't he, descended as he was from a long line of kings?

The fierce nut of pride inside her grew and she found herself pressing hot palms together in her lap. Any woman should be proud to have a man like AJ as her husband, even if he wasn't royal. She could feel a hum of excitement, almost like a wave of heat, rising in the room. Everyone could feel it. She glanced around and saw eyes glowing, cheeks brightening, as AJ carried them all on a tide of emotion. His words echoed like drumbeats around the room, their meaning less important than the man who spoke them and the spell he wove with his powerful voice.

He paused, looked up at the high-beamed ceiling, then started to walk. At first Lani thought he was simply returning to his seat. Disappointment that his performance was over warred with relief that no permanent commitments had been made or broken.

But then he stopped. He turned to his mother—seated only about two feet from Lani—and bowed deeply. Feeling something about to happen, Lani stiffened.

"I am proud—" AJ's voice boomed through the

packed ballroom "—to take up the staff of tradition, and assume the role of king as my father and brother have done before me."

Lani gasped. Everything dimmed a bit and she grasped the arm of her chair to keep a grip on reality.

"And I am pleased to take Lani Rahia as my wife, according to royal custom." His eyes fixed on hers as the last breath fled her lungs. Unable to govern her features into anything but terror-stricken panic, she sat frozen as every eye in the room turned to her.

The faces blurred and she found herself gasping for breath. She felt Priia's soft hand on her arm. "I'm so happy, my daughter." Priia's tear-filled voice penetrated her foggy consciousness. "What a great day this is for Rahiri and for all of us."

Lani tried to say something, but her mouth wouldn't move. How could AJ do this without even consulting her?

Because he was the king, and she was no one. A royal widow, rather like a recently vacated crown, free for the taking and passing on.

Anger prickled through her, battling with the fear. The New Jersey upbringing and the freedoms she'd learned to take for granted challenged the quiet acceptance she'd tried so hard to school in herself.

And AJ had no idea she was pregnant. She felt angry that he hadn't even asked her opinion about the marriage. How would he feel if he knew she carried his brother's child?

If she went along with Priia's plan, he'd never find out. He might suspect something, might wonder at the "premature" baby in such perfect health. He might notice features or traits that fitted his brother better than himself—but he'd never know for sure.

This was one small but deadly advantage women had always had over men. They didn't really know if they were the father of a child. Only the woman held that secret.

"Lani, are you okay?" Priia's voice penetrated the thick fog of her thoughts. "Have some water." She felt a glass pressed to her lips, and she struggled to swallow the cool fluid.

"I…I think so" was all she could manage. She brushed a droplet from her lips, glad that at least she'd managed not to cry. Alarm snapped through her as she saw AJ, climbing the stairs on the dais, moving toward her.

"Stand up, dear," whispered her mother-in-law. She rose shakily to her feet, patting her dress and hoping its creases didn't show any hint of a belly. Every eye in the room felt like a laser searchlight ready to reveal all her fears and misgivings—or were they hopes and dreams?

Majestic in his carriage and bearing, AJ stood in front of her and took her hand. Her fingers trembled in his and heat flushed over her. "Will you take me as your husband?"

Their eyes met—locked onto each other—as he asked the question. It wasn't traditional to ask. He'd done that out of consideration for her.

Or had he? Since she could hardly say no, here amidst the gathered throng of royal admirers.

"I will." Her voice sounded so quiet, so meek, even in the deadly hush of the ballroom. She wondered if AJ would smile, but he didn't. His face, like hers, seemed frozen into a kind of noble mask. Two people acting out roles history had determined for them, and in which emotion and personal opinion played no role.

A cheer rose from the crowd, echoing off the high ceiling and bouncing around the room. Glasses lifted and people began to stamp their feet on the floor, a customary display of enthusiasm.

"Both of you, walk around the room." Priia's urgent whisper penetrated her consciousness.

AJ's arm slipped inside Lani's and drew her down the three stairs to the ballroom floor. The skin of her arm felt hot and feverish against the dark fabric of his jacket. She tried to keep her steps steady, and school her face into an expression of quiet happiness.

AJ's arm felt rigid, tense. He marched with slow dignity, not his usual relaxed gait. No doubt becoming king would turn him into a different person—it already was. Would he become a hard, cold man like Vanu once the wedding vows were sealed?

Cold terror crept through her, tightening her muscles. The stamping feet and calling voices created a blanket of sound that seemed to suck the air from the room and leave her gasping. So much expectation, so many hopes and dreams, and the nation's future hidden in the darkness of her own belly. The pressure weighed on her like a thundercloud and she felt her head becoming light. "I think I'm going to faint," she managed, head tilted toward AJ's powerful jaw.

Her rasped whisper was lost in the roar of the crowd. AJ marched on, oblivious, his face set in a grim smile. Perhaps he'd forgotten she was even there?

The faces started to swirl together, a hot mix of colors with flashes of blackness. Her ankles wobbled and the floor seemed to tilt. She dug her nails into his arm, looking for purchase, and he glanced down.

"I—I don't feel well," she stammered, blinking.

Alarm filled his eyes. "We'll go outside for some air. There's a door over here." He led her past some tables of excited guests, to a side door. Before he left, he turned and bowed. "Please stay and enjoy yourselves."

Seeing that he and Lani were about to leave the room together, the crowd went wild. Perhaps they assumed some kind of romantic action was about to take place. A wave of nausea rose in Lani's throat at the thought that she'd soon be all alone with AJ.

Her future husband.

Outside the door, the cool night air hit her face like a welcome slap. She sucked in a breath and pulled her arm from AJ's, then wondered if she was even allowed to do that.

The lamplight cast AJ's face into shadow, and for a second he looked menacing, unreadable. She didn't know this man but was expected to spend her life with him and sleep in his bed, whether she wanted to or not.

Panic flashed through her and spurred her feet into action. The corridor blurred as she found herself running headlong toward the garden. She didn't know why she was running, only that she had to move—to act on the fierce instinct to flee that reverberated through her whole body.

"Lani, where are you going?" AJ's voice rang after her, and sped her steps. She heard his heels on the stone, marching at first, then jogging along behind her.

Where am I going? The question echoed around her mind as she ran, sandals slapping on the smooth tiles.

There's nowhere to go. The corridor led down to the manicured part of the garden, with a fishpond and perches for the wild birds that ornamented the trees. But its fringes descended into the thick, dense jungle that cloaked the island in its tight embrace. There was no escape.

The stone tiles gave way to grass, cool and damp in the evening dew. She ran a few steps, then felt a strong arm catch her around the waist, almost knocking the breath from her lungs. The baby! If he knew about it he'd never have grabbed her there. But he couldn't know.

She wriggled, instinctively trying to free herself, but his grip was too strong. He wrapped his other arm around her, holding her from behind. "Lani, stop running. We need to talk." Her nerve endings snapped with the desire to run on, but she knew it was hopeless. "I know you're scared but we're in this together."

His deep voice reverberated in her ear, oddly soothing. But she didn't want to say anything. What else could she say but *I'm pregnant.* Yet she'd sworn to keep the baby a secret.

"I didn't intend to spring the whole thing on you. It took me by surprise as well." He turned her in his arms until she stood facing him, no longer pressed against him, but with a couple of inches of warm air between them.

She tried to ignore the strange sensations in her breasts and belly, the odd pulses of desire that only worsened the strange situation. "I thought you were going back to L.A."

That's what she'd hoped for, though she hadn't dared

admit it to herself until just now—when the possibility was gone.

He frowned, features angular in the cool moonlight. "I did, too." He drew in a long breath. "But tonight, surrounded by all those people, the air thick with our island's past and heavy with its future, I knew my place is here. I couldn't shirk my responsibility and still live with myself."

Lani nodded. Again that little kernel of pride throbbed inside her. AJ truly was a man of honor. "Rahiri is lucky to have you," she managed. The words sounded hollow, empty. Shame he wasn't so lucky to have her, a woman who intended to keep a huge thing secret from him for the rest of her life. If she told him, though, he wouldn't be king. She'd break Priia's already suffering heart and put the entire burden of the monarchy's future on herself and her unborn baby. And she'd still be expected to marry again.

AJ's frown deepened. "I'll do my best to be a good husband to you."

He softened his grasp on her arms. He'd been literally holding her in place—preventing her from running off again—and perhaps he realized the grip was at odds with his soothing words.

Lani wobbled slightly on her feet. "I'll do my best to be a good wife." Her words hung in the still night air, the lie echoing off tree trunks and winding itself around them like a vine.

How could she be a good wife if she deceived him about the paternity of the child he'd raise?

Lani's golden eyes shone with anxiety—and why wouldn't they? AJ's chest tightened. This poor girl had no say in her own fate. Of course she could refuse him, but she was far too polite and kind for that. He could have offered to take the crown but refused to marry Lani, but for some reason he knew marrying her was the right thing to do.

Maybe it was that first kiss?

In the kiss all pretense had fallen away. All the tension had evaporated and there was nothing left but… passion. Could that happen again now that they were pledged to each other for life?

Lani's chin tilted high as she met his gaze. She looked so earnest, determined to meet her fate bravely. Everything seemed so awkward.

His synapses tingled as he contemplated kissing her. Perhaps that would cut through all the layers of ceremony and nerves and anticipation and jump-start the connection he'd felt between them that first night. "I have an idea."

Dark lashes lowered, she looked coyly away, like a young girl who'd never been kissed. But he knew better. Somewhere beneath that demure surface lurked a smoldering cauldron of passion that he ached to taste again.

"What?" she murmured, daring to glance up.

He replied by lowering his face to hers. He did it slowly, to give her a chance to react and respond in her own time. At first she flinched slightly, as if to dodge him, then she seemed to steel herself and tilted her lips to his.

Their lips met like opposing magnets coming together, pulled by an unseen force. A shock wave of desire crashed through AJ as Lani's mouth opened to greet his. Her body softened and he wrapped his arms around her, hugging her close. Heat gathered between them and his skin hummed with awareness of her body. His fingers itched to tug at the embroidered fabric of her dress and pull it away to reveal smooth, golden skin.

Her mouth tasted like warm honey, delicious and inviting. He deepened the kiss, trailing his fingers down her spine. Lani kissed him back, tongue reaching for his, her arms wrapped around his waist and her slim body straining against him.

But something was different.

Her actions lacked the sense of raw abandon he remembered from their first kiss. No breathless moans pierced the night air. Her fingertips pressed into the muscles of his back, but with a forced quality, not the fevered intensity he remembered.

He pulled away slowly. Lani's eyes opened, and he noted their look of curious alarm. Did she wonder if she'd put on a good enough show of passion?

AJ fought the urge to frown. It didn't help that they were out here in the dark garden, while all the guests still drank and talked inside. "Let's go somewhere more comfortable." Then they could talk in private and get more used to their new situation.

"Okay." She blinked. Quiet and accommodating as usual. Would he ever know what went on in her mind, behind that polite smile?

He took her arm and they walked down the corridor. "We won't be missed at the party. They'll have more fun talking about us if we're not there." He shot her a smile.

"Yes." Her arm felt rigid in his.

AJ led her through the lamplit passages of the private

quarters of the palace and into his private sitting room. It adjoined the bedroom; no one would come to disturb them here. The guests would stay until dawn, then stumble drunkenly to their chauffeured cars.

Priia had redecorated the room in his absence, in a simple, masculine style that he rather liked. No doubt now he'd be expected to move into the royal bedchamber, but there was no way he'd spend the night in a room where Lani had once slept with Vanu.

He gestured to a low chaise covered in soft leather. Lani perched stiffly on the edge of it.

"Would you like some wine?" He gestured to the stocked bar in one corner.

"No, thanks. I'm fine." Her rushed response surprised him. He moved to the cabinet and poured a glass for himself. He sat next to Lani on the sofa, each of them upright, formal, painfully separate. Even his favorite vintage tasted slightly bitter on his tongue.

What had he got himself into?

He set his glass down. "You don't have to marry me, you know."

Lani's gaze snapped to meet his. "But of course I want to." The gleam of panic in her eyes warred with her reassuring words.

"I know my mom has probably put a lot of pressure on you, and now I've piled on some more by publicly declaring I'd marry you, but I don't intend to force you into anything. If you want to call it off, just say the word."

He braced himself for her response. Her rejection.

The events of tonight had lit a fire inside him—a fire of warm ancient traditions and comforting rituals, and he'd committed to keeping that fire alive. The prospect of spending his life with the beautiful Lani had suddenly seemed to be one of the sweeter benefits of taking up the role his country expected of him.

Even now, her golden gaze sent a charge of electricity snaking through him, and his fingertips ached to roam over her soft skin.

But not if she didn't want him. He had more than enough women after him back in L.A. There was no reason on earth good enough to force a woman into bed with him if she didn't want to be there.

"I don't want to call it off." Lani's words came out in a staccato rhythm. "I want to get married as soon as possible." She wiped her palms on the shimmering fabric of her evening dress.

AJ cocked his head. "Then why do you look so damned unhappy about it?"

"I am happy, really." She reached out to him and wrapped her arms stiffly around him. The goose bumps on her arms rasped his skin.

"You have a funny way of showing it." Still, the hopeful gesture warmed his heart. He turned and put his arm around her. Only to find that she was shivering, her whole body tense and rigid.

He raised a thumb to her cheek and stroked it. "You need to relax."

"I know. I'm just…excited."

Panicked, more like. Maybe she was afraid he'd want to make love to her tonight? "We don't have to rush into anything."

"Oh, but we should. Everyone is expecting it." Something flashed in her eyes, panic, or calculation, he couldn't tell which. Curiosity unfurled in him like a flame.

He tilted his head and held her gaze. "You think they expect us to sleep together?"

"Probably, yes." She nodded.

He lifted a brow. Heat flared in his groin. "Do you think we should?"

Her cheek heated under his thumb. "Yes, I do." Her voice was low, breathy.

AJ blinked. He'd not expected that answer. In fact he'd had no intention of doing more than kiss her for now. But maybe she wanted to get such a big milestone out of the way? Or to make sure he was a considerate lover before she committed the rest of her life to him? There were many possible explanations, under the bizarre circumstances.

And since he was a healthy male, any one of them would do. He rose from the sofa, and took her hand. "Then I guess we'd better go into the bedroom."

Five

Lani followed AJ, her hand in his. She could do this. It was best for Rahiri, and for the family. AJ would be king, his mom would be happy, and her child would be free to grow to adulthood before taking on the responsibilities and pressures of the monarchy.

AJ turned to her on the threshold and took both her hands in his. "Are you sure?"

She hesitated. He was truly a thoughtful man, one who deserved a better woman than she. But if Priia's plan was to succeed she must…do the deed with him at the earliest opportunity.

Do the deed. Even the phrase suggested a crime, but she couldn't really call it "making love" under circumstances like this.

Making love. She'd never done that with Vanu, either. No love had existed between them, though she'd certainly tried hard to find some in the first few months—before she'd realized Vanu had no love lurking anywhere inside him.

AJ stroked her cheek again, which made her shiver slightly. A warm shiver of pleasure. His touch was gentle, encouraging, his big hands sensitive. Lani lifted her own fingers and gingerly caressed his shirtfront. Thick muscle rose to greet her fingertips through the crisp, black surface.

He had a sensational body. She'd seen him swimming in the lagoon one morning while she was on her way to breakfast. Her heart had almost stopped beating at the sight of his broad shoulders gleaming in the morning sun while water licked over his sturdy, bronzed physique.

Desire rose inside her, trickling up from her core. She could do this. And enjoy it.

AJ's hands reached for the sash at her waist and pulled carefully at the elaborate knot. She helped him get it undone and the thick strip of silk fell to the floor at her feet. He stroked her back, then put his hands on either side of her waist, caressing her through her dress.

Her breath caught. What if he felt her belly and noticed it was no longer flat? It wasn't very round, but in the last couple of days there was a noticeable bump.

Guilt forked through her and she plucked at the buttons of his shirt. Better to get on with things and get him so wrapped up in the act that he didn't notice anything strange about her body.

And he thought she was so *nice*.

Her heart hammered wildly as she pulled his black tunic away from his skin, revealing his smooth, strong chest. Her nipples tightened, straining against her bra, and her insides seemed to twist into a knot. Was this excitement okay for the baby? She knew sex was supposed to be fine during pregnancy, but somehow it seemed wrong to feel pleasure under the circumstances.

AJ's dark eyes met hers as she glanced up at his face. He smiled. "I think I might be the luckiest man alive."

Lani swallowed. No, the luckiest man alive would have a wife who was honest and open, not one who needed to have sex with him as soon as possible so it would look like her child was his.

She dropped her gaze to the button on his pants, and worked at it. Her fingers sprang away as if stung when she noticed the thick, hard arousal hiding beneath the zipper.

AJ laughed. "As you can see, I'm quite attracted to you."

She managed to smile. "And I to you." An understatement. Her insides pulsed with arousal and somewhere deep inside her ached in a way she'd never felt before.

AJ unfastened her dress—a single hook held the whole thing together—and pulled it carefully away from her skin.

The warm night air caressed her, but as she stood there, naked before him, an ache of longing opened inside her. A deep, cold loneliness that craved something—sex, love, companionship—all the things that had never come together in her life before.

Now this kind and handsome man offered her all those things and more.

Tears sprang to her eyes and a sob tore from her throat.

"What's the matter?" AJ moved his hands from her waist to her shoulders, where he held her steady. He frowned, no doubt getting irritated by her hot-and-cold behavior. "Is being my wife such an awful fate?"

Another sob shook her from head to toe. "I can't do this." Tears fell from her cheeks and dripped onto her bare breasts.

"Then you won't. We'll get dressed. I'm not going to push you into anything."

Lani froze. "But we have to." The shrill sound of her own voice startled her.

AJ frowned and shoved a hand through his hair. "Why?"

"Because I'm already pregnant."

Her words rang in the air like the clash of a ceremonial gong. AJ frowned, trying to process the information. "You're carrying Vanu's baby." His gaze dropped to her stomach, then her hands flew to cover it.

She nodded, eyes filled with tears.

A horrible, cold sensation settled over AJ. Just when he'd finally committed himself to this new life, when he'd chosen to marry Lani, and was looking forward to sharing his life with her…his brother's long, strong and deadly arm reached out to him from beyond the grave.

"Why didn't you say anything before?"

Lani shuddered. "I didn't know until a few days ago. Then I took a test, and…" She looked down, apparently unable to meet his gaze.

AJ stared at her. He couldn't understand the secrecy. His mom was so anxious for them to marry, to keep the family together in the traditional way. Maybe they'd decided he'd be less likely to marry her if he knew she was carrying Vanu's baby.

"So you thought you'd marry me and pretend the child is mine?"

"I didn't want to…" She swallowed. Lani looked like she wanted to say more, but couldn't.

"But my mom put you up to it."

She nodded. "She said it would be better because then you would be the next in line to the throne, and not the baby."

AJ spun away and blew out a curse. "I can't believe you women cooked this up. I've never been hungry for the throne. I'd have been quite happy to leave and let your child rule Rahiri."

"I think that's what your mom was afraid of. She wants you here."

He knew. Her obvious happiness at having him back home had been a source of guilt and torment to him—until he'd decided to stay.

"What about you?" He peered at her through narrowed eyes. "You don't need to marry me. Either way your child will inherit the throne."

"My child's not even born yet."

"Your child's not even showing yet." AJ's eyes raked over her belly. "And at this point I'm not even sure whether to believe you now. Get dressed."

The command startled her into action and she picked her dress up off the floor and pulled it back on. AJ buttoned his pants and turned away. If she really was pregnant and wanted to pretend it was his, no wonder she'd been so anxious to have sex right away. Desire had nothing to do with it.

Revulsion and anger flashed through him. She'd seemed so sweet and innocent—now he knew she was anything but. Lovely Lani had schemed to lure him into a lifetime of deception.

He'd never wanted to come back here. His gut instincts had told him to leave as soon as possible. If anything the instinct had become even stronger after his explosive kiss with Lani. He should have known her pretty facade hid a dangerous and deceptive core. What kind of woman would kiss another man when her husband was barely gone?

He peered at her, hating her beauty and the mix of fear and alarm in her wide, golden eyes.

He turned from her and strode across the room. He should never have promised to stay. It went against everything he wanted from his own life. He loved his film career and his group of friends in L.A. He had no interest in getting married and settling down into some routine existence.

But the ancient ceremonial drumbeats had stirred something lying dormant in his blood. They'd kicked his heart into a primal rhythm and drawn him back into the mysterious and powerful pull these islands exerted over anyone who'd lived here. The magic of the lush jungle and the bright, clear ocean formed a paradise of beauty that could entice any man, much like a stunning woman.

Seductive—and dangerous, in that you never knew what hit you until it was too late. Until you were trapped, bound by tradition and the expectations of people you didn't even know.

Well, no more. He'd weakened for a moment and taken up the mantle they all wanted to thrust on him, but he could throw it off just as easily.

He turned to Lani, who stood just to the side of the wide bed, already rumpled by their almost-lovemaking.

She'd said she was so happy, that she wanted to climb in that bed with him.

All lies.

"You disgust me."

She flinched slightly, as if his words stung her. "I'm sorry."

"More lies. You're not sorry, or you wouldn't have done it."

"I did tell you the truth."

"I'm sure you have your own motives for that choice, too." Perhaps the prospect of bedding a man she didn't love—or even like—had proved too much for even her hardened sensibilities? "No doubt you've decided that marriage to your husband's brother is too much to stomach—tradition be damned."

She blinked. "I'm willing to marry you."

AJ let out a growl. "Willing? How kind of you to be so generous with your life. With your body. Allow me to throw your sacrifice back at you. Please leave." He gestured to the door, hand shaking with fury. Her wide-eyed desire of only a few minutes ago was so obviously fake, and it disgusted him that she'd tried to trap him into sex with her when she viewed the entire arrangement as a chore.

But she didn't move.

"Leave." His command echoed off the walls, and no doubt out into the night since the windows were open.

Lani seemed to shrink a little. She gathered her dress about her. "The guests are probably still here."

"Then what are you worried about? That they'll see you in a state of undress and assume you've been in my bed? I thought that was what you wanted." He narrowed his eyes. "Or was that only when you intended to trick them into thinking your baby was mine. It doesn't look so good if you sleep with me when you're pregnant with my brother's baby, does it?"

She shook her head. "I didn't want any of this." Tears welled in her eyes.

"Me, either, but you at least chose your role by marrying my brother. I got shoved into this dog-and-pony show from the moment I was born. It took me years to work my way out of it and I almost made the biggest mistake of my life letting you and my mom suck me back into it with trickery and deception. With a face like that I'd imagine you're used to getting your own way."

Her tear-filled gaze only fueled the indignation pricking his muscles. "I told you to go."

If she didn't get out of here, he might get suckered in by some sob story she'd cook up. She still clutched her dress awkwardly about her. He grabbed her sash off the floor and thrust it at her; his fingers instinctively flinching back from hers as she took it. Her touch was deadly and her wanted her out of sight and mind before anything else could happen.

Less than an hour ago he'd promised to stay and take his place as king here. Filled with ancestral pride and hope for the future, he'd enjoyed the sense of comradeship and even destiny as people welcomed him home.

Under false pretenses. There was already a new king or queen waiting to take the throne, hidden beneath the rumpled folds of Lani's dress.

She struggled with the sash, wrapping its length about her still-slim waist. He wondered if there really was a baby. Perhaps this was her last-ditch effort to send him running? He didn't know what to believe anymore. Confusion and anger warred inside him. He was used to being the director, setting up the action, telling people what to do. If something didn't work out he could fix it in post-production—ruthlessly cutting and even reshooting if needed.

There were no retakes in real life.

Her sash now retied, Lani slipped on her sandals. Her fingers shook—and that stirred a trace of pity in his heart.

He crushed it quickly and moved to open the door. From down the corridor he could hear voices, the sound of feet on the stone. Revelers leaving the party. What kind of scandal would it cause for Lani to run past them, eyes filled with tears?

Surely they'd expect no less from a grieving widow forced into marriage with a man she barely knew. Nothing about this situation was pretty.

Lani hesitated in the doorway, plucking nervously at her silk dress.

"Can't face them?" His voice was cold. "Maybe you could just tell them the truth, like you did with me."

She hadn't said a word for some time and her silence was starting to rub him raw. Who was she to stand there looking so innocent and hard-done-by? Suddenly he was the bad guy, the one who threatened to ruin everyone's careful plans.

Lani's lips quivered before she finally spoke. "Your mom wants to keep it a secret."

"Do you do everything she tells you?"

Her silence answered his question.

Irritation flashed over him. "She needs to learn that you can't manipulate people like puppets." Maybe that's where Vanu got it from. He'd certainly pulled the strings in their world from behind the scenes. It was time for someone to snap the strings right off. He grabbed her arm, hating the way his skin heated when he touched her. "Come on, let's get this charade over with."

Lani pulled her arm back. Not wanting to get into a wrestling match, he let it go. "It was such a happy evening for your mother."

AJ frowned. He could still hear the hypnotic drumbeats somewhere in the distance. People were dancing and laughing and enjoying the vision of the future they'd all conjured together such a short time earlier.

"Your mom's been so sad lately. Can't we let her enjoy her party?" She didn't meet his gaze.

"Let the happy charade continue and ignore reality for another day?" His muscles tightened. "Why not? But I don't think that should extend to keeping you in my room all night." He shot her a harsh look. "It's a little too crowded in here with you and your baby."

Not to mention your dead husband. He didn't say that, though. He wasn't totally insensitive.

"Would you mind escorting me along the corridor?" She said it softly, still not lifting her eyes to his. Very Rahiian and traditional. "Everyone will know something's wrong if they see me by myself."

He was tempted to say no. Everything was wrong; it was better people should find out. This whole pretense sickened him. And he hated the way Lani's soft voice tugged at his sympathies and made him want to save her from humiliation.

How could she be so infuriating and still so beautiful at the same time? Her skin glowed in the soft light from the wall sconces, and her hair shimmered like gold thread. "Sure," he growled.

He did not touch her this time. No need to feel heat

flash over his skin where there should be revulsion. He marched down the corridor with Lani hurrying along beside him in her long dress. Lani's room was on the other side of the palace, past the area where the party was still taking place. Laughter and music spilled into the hallway as they marched on. Groups stood chatting in the hallway outside the ballroom, smiling as they approached.

AJ's insides contracted. All these people now saw them as the happy couple with a bright future ahead of them.

If they only knew.

"So serious, Arun." An older man he recognized as one of his father's ministers smiled at him. "Already the weight of responsibility is carving lines into your face."

He attempted to soften what must be quite a scowl. "I'm just escorting Lani back to her room. She's tired." He didn't have to make up stories.

"I'm sure she is." He didn't wiggle his eyebrows but the implication was there. AJ saw a slight flush rise to Lani's cheeks.

She should be embarrassed. That's exactly what she'd wanted. Now everyone thought they'd sealed their pact with wild lovemaking. He cursed the desire that still coursed through his body at the sight of her. All his instincts had told him to stay far, far away from Lani and everything she represented.

They'd been right.

"Your mother is so happy, Arun. What joy you're bringing to all our people." The former minister's wife patted his forearm. "And I've never seen a lovelier couple."

The last remark was addressed to Lani, who replied, "You're sweet, but I really must get some rest."

Her smile made her look so innocent and adorable. They had no idea why she needed rest.

AJ's tension eased slightly as they moved away from the excited guests and down the dimly lit corridor away from the ballroom. He had no intention of returning this way and facing innuendo about exactly what he and Lani had been up to. He'd rather traverse the pitch-dark garden.

Lani now walked ahead of him, shoulders tight under the fall of hair cascading to her waist.

Just a half hour ago he'd run his fingers though that silken mass and imagined them as partners—husband and wife. That idea had evaporated like the dawn mist, and now she again seemed like a semi-hostile stranger.

When she reached her room, Lani turned and fixed wide, worried eyes on him. "Thank you for helping me run the gauntlet."

"I don't know why I did." He cocked his head. "Obviously I'm a soft touch."

"You're not. You're a man of honor and that's evident in everything you've said and done so far." Her voice was steady and she leveled a clear gaze at him. "You should be king and it's a terrible shame if I've somehow ruined that."

Her words stopped his negative thoughts in their tracks. No one cared what Lani really wanted. She was expected to do whatever it took to ease the succession and make life easy for other people. None of this was her idea. What did she have to gain from sleeping with him, let alone marrying him? She'd probably rather be curled up with a good book and some saltines.

"Why did you agree to go along with my mom's plot to trick me into marrying you even though you're already pregnant with the heir?"

"She didn't know I was pregnant when you first came. I didn't, either. I found out that first night, when I was ill and left dinner early."

Things started to fall into place.

He frowned when he realized that first passionate kiss had come before she knew about the baby. "So the wheels driving us into marriage were already rolling and you figured it was too late to stop them?"

"Your mom was so excited about you staying. And I liked the idea of my child being able to enjoy being a kid, without the pressure of already being a monarch. On some level the idea made sense, until…"

"Until you tried to get naked with me. Then there was nothing to hide behind."

"I'm not cut out for deception." She met his gaze with a hard stare of her own. Then it softened. "And you don't deserve that. You're a good man."

Her ridiculously long hair fell about her shoulders. Her oddly shaped traditional dress didn't hold together well without the sash. Those big eyes still brimmed with tears that glittered in her thick lashes. He fought a powerful urge to take her in his arms and comfort her.

Was he angry with her or at the unfortunate effect she had on him? She was just trying to do what everyone wanted of her. Tradition had shoved her between a rock and a hard place and he couldn't help wondering which one he was. "I am glad you told me."

"I couldn't have lived with myself if I didn't." She held her neat chin high.

"Why would you put up with marrying a stranger in the first place?"

She looked away for a moment. "For Rahiri." She looked back at him, expression serious. "And for your mom. You can see how happy everyone is to have you back."

He shoved a hand through his hair and let out a bitter laugh. "So you have every reason to marry me except… me."

Her cheeks darkened. "I'd have been proud to have you as my husband."

AJ shook his head. "Proud. I'm not sure that's entirely the sentiment I'd hope for in my wife, but it's an interesting one."

Lani swallowed, obviously embarrassed by her unsatisfactory response. "I am attracted to you." Her shy whisper made a chuckle rise in his throat, and sent a jolt of lust to his groin.

"I'm grateful for that, at least." He cocked his head. "I wouldn't want to marry a woman who finds me repugnant." He crossed his arms, trying to not be seduced by the rather dazed expression on her too-beautiful face. "So you were prepared to put up with me for the sake of Rahiri."

She shrugged, and for the first time a sparkle of humor lit her eyes. "I figured I could handle it."

"Your willingness to do your patriotic duty is impressive." He couldn't stop a smile hovering at the corners of his mouth. Then he remembered she'd intended to pretend her child was his. Her traditional dress concealed her shape. "How far along are you?"

Her face tightened. "Almost two months."

"You conceived right before Vanu disappeared?"

She nodded. "That's why I didn't know I was pregnant. When I felt ill, or tired, I just thought it was stress."

"Vanu never knew about the baby."

"No." She held his gaze a little too boldly, as if she expected him to read something into that.

He wasn't sure what to think. They'd been married for nearly five years, so why did she only become pregnant now? It was odd, unsettling. Too...convenient, somehow. "No one would have ever known it wasn't my baby if you hadn't told me."

"I would have known." Something glittered in her eyes. Determination, perhaps, or some of that steely strength hidden under her pretty exterior. Desire rose again inside him, a simmering flash of heat that warred with his anger at the deception.

"I appreciate your honesty." He hesitated, thoughts weaving themselves in his brain even as warmth rose through his body. When he'd stated his intent to become king, he'd meant it. Tradition and honor now pumped through his heart along with his red blood cells. Suddenly it had seemed as if his whole life had led up to this night, when he assumed the responsibilities of leadership. He'd marshaled casts of hundreds, managed budgets and planned for contingencies. He knew how to deal with crises and manage difficult people and situations. The result, so far, had been about ninety minutes of entertainment for anyone who cared to watch, but as king of Rahiri he'd have the power to shape lives through investment in education and infrastructure.

Lani wasn't the only reason he'd decided to stay. And now she wouldn't be the reason he'd leave. "Maybe your little revelation doesn't have to ruin everything."

She blinked. "No?"

"Don't play the innocent, now." He laughed. "You know what I mean. We could still get married."

Her cheeks reddened. "Even now that you know?"

"It's a baby." He shrugged. He could raise a child. What did it matter if it was his biological child or not? He'd never given much thought to family life, but the prospect held some appeal.

And he couldn't deny that Lani held considerable appeal, too. Brave as well as beautiful, she'd risked everything to tell him the truth. Surely he could take a risk on a woman like that if it meant fulfilling the role everyone seemed so desperate for him to take on.

"I'm excited about having a baby." Her face brightened. "I've been longing for one for years. It's like a dream come true…" Her lips faltered. "Just at the wrong time."

He wanted to ask why it had taken so long to conceive, but he held his tongue. Instead he said, "I'm not afraid of raising my brother's baby."

A dark shard of worry sliced into his mind. What if Vanu's baby was like Vanu? He fought off the nasty thought.

AJ flexed the muscles in his back. They suddenly felt tight, maybe under the weight of so many expectations. "So the child would never know?"

"Things could get complicated because of royal succession."

"I suppose we could tell him when he came of age, but I can see how it makes more sense to keep it quiet. When we decide it's time for him to become king, I can quietly step aside."

"Yes, then there's no real need for him or anyone else to know."

"And he won't be traumatized by finding out as an

adult. It does make more sense." AJ rubbed his temples, which throbbed slightly. In one evening he'd decided to change his whole life and embrace a new one—now suddenly he'd taken on fatherhood, too. A curse fell from his lips.

"What?" Lani looked alarmed.

"I'm suddenly on the brink of being a father, and I never even got to enjoy your naked body. That seems a real shame."

Lani blushed. "Sorry I ruined everything."

"You did the right thing. There'll be plenty of time to catch up later—with no tears, I hope." He paused and studied her face. "If we do get married, that is."

Doubt still swirled in his mind and heart. Everything had happened so quickly, and with such deadly finality. Each decision he made seemed a matter of life and death.

"I'm not going to pressure you into anything." Lani spoke softly, gazing off to one side. "I never wanted to. It's your decision, and now you have all the facts."

AJ took in a deep breath and straightened his shoulders. "I committed myself to Rahiri tonight, and to you, and I stand by my decision." Conviction filled his heart. "Your courage in choosing to tell the truth gives me every reason to trust you as my wife."

Lani blinked, obviously embarrassed by his words. Her cheeks still shone like roses.

"But you really are far too beautiful for your own good." He managed a snarl as he said it.

Lani shrugged and shot him a wry smile. "That's what my aunt Freda used to say. She said girls like me end up in trouble."

"And you did." She looked startled, eyes suddenly wider. "By joining the Rahiian royal family, I mean.

Life in the palace isn't all eating bonbons and being fanned by faithful servants."

"No, there are the big parties, the long banquets. It's exhausting." A smile brightened her eyes for the first time since her revelation.

"Lucky thing we're both young and strong enough to handle it." AJ found his hands once again itching to reach out to her. "Maybe we can make a go of this marriage thing. Heck, we might even enjoy it."

Her eyes shone in the dim light of the bedroom. AJ picked up one of the hands dangling at her side, and pressed its softness between his palms. "The more I get to know you, the more I like you."

She bit her lip. "And I like you, too. That's why I couldn't lie to you."

He frowned. "The big question is whether we can lie to everyone else."

"For some reason that doesn't bother me." Lani's smooth brow furrowed slightly. "It's no one else's business where our child comes from. It's between you and me that the truth is important."

AJ stared at her. "You know, that makes perfect sense. If we're married, it's *our* child. Vanu's gone and he's not coming back, so he's not being cheated out of anything. We'll raise the baby as ours, with all the love and affection we'd shower on any child we have."

Lani's hand stiffened. She bit her lip, then peered into his eyes. "I just had a thought. What if we do have more children and you find yourself wanting the oldest child that really is yours to inherit the throne instead? Things could get complicated."

AJ stared at her for a moment, trying to understand her dilemma, then he laughed. "I'm not an Egyptian pharoah with a desire to dominate the world. I will certainly not start interfering in matters of succession other than by bowing out for the next person to take over."

Lani's smile returned. "I had to ask, but I believe you. You don't seem like that type."

Though Vanu would have been. The unpleasant thought pierced the warm mist of happiness that had drifted back into the room.

AJ picked up Lani's hand and kissed it, trying to dispel the image of Vanu that hovered suddenly in his consciousness. Would his cruel older brother haunt him for the rest of his days as he raised his child?

Lani's hands, so soft and scented like lilies, filled his senses. She sighed as he pressed his lips to them.

No. Vanu could not cast darkness over his life from beyond the grave. He was dead and gone, in the past, and AJ would let him stay there. He and Lani would make a bright future for themselves and their child.

He lowered her hands and looked into her eyes. Mysteries glistened in their golden depths. He didn't know where this marriage would lead them, but the adventure invited him to climb aboard. He kissed her softly, his lips just brushing hers.

Lani tilted her chin, pressing her mouth to his as her lashes lowered. AJ wound his arms around her slim back, holding her close. Tension fled his muscles as he let himself sink into her softness. She sighed and writhed gently against him, her passion natural and soft, not like earlier when she'd seemed—desperate.

He let his fingers roam lower, to cup her firm backside and caress her long, elegant thighs. Fantasies of having those thighs wrapped around him heated his blood. Lani's fingers dived into his hair and slid under his collar, making his skin hum with arousal. He could feel her nipples tighten under her dress, and he knew she was aroused, too.

His fingers prickled with the desire to peel off her silk gown and bare her golden skin, but a powerful instinct deep in his gut told him to wait. He pulled back a few inches and smoothed her dress. Her belly quivered slightly beneath his touch.

Lani was recently widowed, pregnant and obviously alarmed and confused by the strange dilemma she'd found herself in. This evening's events were enough to give anyone whiplash, and he didn't want to rush headlong into steamy sex— Well, he did, but that would only make the situation even more explosive and unpredictable.

He needed to be strong for both of them. "I'll sleep here in your bed tonight." She blinked at him, those golden eyes still wary. "But we won't make love."

Her cheeks flushed. Relief or disappointment? It didn't matter. Or maybe it was the word *love*—so strange and inappropriate under the forced circumstances that pushed them together.

When he made love to Lani for the first time it would be right. He had the rest of his life to enjoy his bride, and for tonight he'd put her needs before his own.

"You sleep on this side." He pulled back the covers. She climbed in, still in her dress. "And I'll sleep on the other."

Six

Lani managed a few hours of fitful sleep. It was hard to relax when your life kept changing so drastically from minute to minute, let alone next to a man who stirred your senses and scrambled your thoughts. AJ had gone to the gym early, as usual, and she showered and changed in her own room, with growing anxiety. Her mother-in-law had no idea she'd told AJ about the baby, or that the revelation had almost sent him packing and she didn't relish telling her.

At the breakfast table, Priia beamed, half-hidden behind a stack of newspapers from around the region. "Front-page story in every one!"

Lani glanced at the *Aipu Clarion*. The story directly beneath the announcement of Rahiri's new king declared that a newborn goat on a neighboring island had shown evidence of magic powers. "Are we on the front of the *New York Times?*"

Priia waved her hand dismissively, which caused her gold bracelets to jangle. "They probably haven't even woken up yet. Besides, those big papers prefer bad news to happy news like ours." She leaned in, eyes wide. "How are you feeling?"

"Fine." Lani spooned some pineapple onto her plate.

"Not too exhausted after last night?" She winked her mascara-encrusted lashes.

Lani gulped and lowered her voice to a whisper. "I told AJ about the baby."

"What?" Priia's shriek pierced the air. She spun around and looked relieved that no servants were nearby. She grasped Lani's hand. "Why?"

"It was too big a thing to lie to my future husband about." She sat close to Priia. "He was shocked at first, but glad that I'd told him."

Manicured fingernails dug into her skin. "He's still willing to go ahead with the marriage?"

Lani nodded. "He seemed okay with it after we talked."

Priia let out a huge sigh and released her grip on Lani's wrist. "Thank heavens! Oh, my goodness. You were brave. Or crazy, I'm not sure which." She fluffed her hair. "Of course, I'm not surprised that he was still willing to do the right thing."

Tension cramped Lani's muscles. Everything was so complicated. "He's agreed to keep the baby's parentage quiet so that he can become king."

"Perfect." Priia rose to her feet. "Better than I could have hoped for. You truly are a gift, my dear." She kissed Lani's cheeks and swept from the room.

Lani was eating a piece of melon when AJ walked in, a guarded expression on his face. "I'm not sure if I had a night of violent and colorful dreams or if I made a lot of very bold promises last night."

"The evidence is in the papers." She pointed to the stack. "If it's on the covers of *The Napau Inquirer*, then it must be true." The cover photo of them both, snapped right after his announcement, showed the look of surprise and terror on her face. Hopefully people would take it for delight.

AJ raised a brow, then frowned. "*King AJ.* It doesn't really roll off the tongue, does it?"

She laughed. "I don't know why not. Half the names in Rahiri are barely pronounceable. And as king, you get to make the rules, anyway."

"There's a comforting thought."

A waiter whisked in with AJ's favorite breakfast—two slices of French toast with crispy bacon—and another stack of papers.

AJ grabbed a magazine off the top. "Made *The Hollywood Reporter.* 'Dragon Chaser Helmer Catches a Crown.' Makes it sound a bit like a Frisbee, doesn't it?" he said as he sunk into a chair. "Oddly enough, the crown's sitting pretty easy on my head this morning." He tilted his head and peered at her with those seductive dark eyes. "That may have to do with the lovely lady that comes along with it."

She felt her face heat as a smile crept across her face. At least they hadn't actually made love last night. That would have definitely been too much too soon. Her attraction to him was alarming under the circumstances.

AJ's phone rang. "Ugh, not again. I've been besieged by phone calls since before dawn. Mostly from people who work with me. They're all afraid they'll be out of a job."

He took the call, reassuring someone that he had every intention of completing his next movie, but he couldn't talk details right now.

Lani poured him some tea and waited until he put the phone away. "Tell them they'll just have to move to Rahiri."

"Yeah. Maybe I'll open a studio here, get all those bigwig execs to fly to me rather than the other way around."

"Your mom's always trying to pump the tourism industry here."

"What tourism industry?"

"True, but maybe this is Rahiri's big chance to finally land on the world map. Direct flights from London and Paris, five-star hotels, celebrity guests." She winked.

"Don't get her started, I beg you." AJ leaned back in his chair. "One thing at a time. The possibilities do seem pretty limitless right now, though, don't they?"

Media swarmed the palace, first the local TV stations and then the entertainment shows from L.A. and beyond, all intrigued by the Hollywood playboy about to become king.

At first Priia tried to fob them off with bright announcements of her own and warnings that the happy couple were "busy," but by the afternoon, it was obvious that a press conference was in order and they scheduled it for the following morning. Priia suggested Lani wear a pretty, pale-yellow dress with shimmering embroidery. She attempted to deck AJ out in a colorful ceremonial tunic, but he managed to mollify her by wearing an Armani suit.

"What a stunning couple!" she exclaimed. "Of

course they all want pictures, and they must have them."

"I'll bet they're also looking for some dirt to dish," murmured AJ. Lani had tried to ignore the same dark thought. Happy news didn't sell nearly as well as disaster.

"Just hold your chin high and remember the proud history of our island." Priia stroked her tall son's cheek.

"Thanks for the advice, Mom." AJ shot Lani a mischievous glance. Lani had noticed that AJ usually gave his mom lip service, then did whatever he wanted.

"And Lani, if they ask you too much, tell them you're still mourning. Don't let them upset you."

Lani gulped. Hopefully AJ would do most of the talking.

Priia's main assistant put her head around the door. "They're waiting for you on the veranda. I served them tea and coconut stars just as you suggested."

"Wonderful." Priia clapped her hands. "Then they'll all be in a good mood. Come on, my dears. Let's give them a glimpse of Rahiri's gorgeous new royal family."

They stepped out on the veranda, and Lani froze when she saw how many people had gathered. At least fifty, many of them with cameras pressed to their faces. Voices began chattering, reporters reeling off live commentary, as she and AJ took their seats under some very hot, rapidly erected lights.

Microphones thrust toward them. "AJ, how does it feel to marry your brother's wife?"

Lani blanched. AJ leaned back in his chair, confident and relaxed. "I don't know. We're not married yet."

"You're leaving a lot of broken-hearted women

behind in L.A.," quipped one rather flamboyant reporter. "Do you feel you're ready to settle down?"

"Absolutely."

"I can see why," declared a bold female reporter. "Your fiancée is stunning." She pointed her mike right at Lani. "How do you feel about taking a new husband when you've barely had a chance to mourn the first one?"

Lani cleared her throat. "It's traditional."

"But surely, in the twenty-first century, some traditions seem a little barbaric."

AJ grasped her hand firmly. "No one is forcing Lani and me into this marriage. We're both pleased to hold our family together in the way chosen by our ancestors."

"Give us a kiss, then!" coaxed an older male reporter with a British accent.

Lani shrank into her chair. Could they really expect them to put on a show for the cameras?

"Please don't offend my bride's royal dignity." AJ managed a tone that was both formal and jesting. "And give us a chance to get the relationship off the ground at our own speed."

"There must be pressure on you to produce an heir to the throne, since your brother didn't."

Lani gulped. It was hard to resist pointing out there was one on the way already.

"None whatsoever. We're young and strong and will be here for a long time to come." His cheery retort soothed her.

"Lani, is it disturbing to you that Vanu's body has never been found?" A young female reporter thrust a microphone at her.

She stiffened. "I've accepted the fact that it may

never be found. We all searched long and hard for his boat, but found no sign of it. The ocean is deep and keeps many secrets."

She could never let *anyone* know the deadly secret that she was relieved Vanu was gone.

Reporters clustered around the palace all day, hoping to snap a candid shot of the couple. AJ's celebrity status had turned the story into a hot property, and the internet buzzed with speculation and innuendo about the arranged marriage. Once pictures of Lani hit the media, revealing that she was not only royal but also strikingly beautiful, interest only grew.

Lani peeped out behind the closed wooden shutters. "Do you think we'll ever be able to go outside again without being photographed?"

"They'll lose interest eventually." AJ spoke while thumbing a message on his BlackBerry. "Something more dramatic will happen."

"What are you going to do about the movie you're supposed to edit in a couple of weeks?" There were so many things they still hadn't talked about. Did AJ think he could continue his Hollywood career and rule Rahiri at the same time?

"The editor can start work without me. He has the script and storyboard with my notes, and of course we can videoconference. As things progress we'll make new plans. I signed up for the job and I don't shirk a commitment."

"Which is why you're still here." She looked up, suddenly shy. AJ appeared so strong, invincible, even. But how much of this whole experience had he not thought through yet? He was obviously trying hard to do the right thing. But what if he wasn't ready to give up the thrills and excitement of his life in L.A.?

She couldn't help thinking about those "broken-hearted" beauties he'd left behind. Who was he texting? Already a little thread of jealousy twisted inside her. She rose to her feet and paced along the wall of shuttered windows.

AJ looked up. "I'm restless, too. Let's go out for a walk."

"With the entire press corps following us?"

He rose to his feet, tall and handsome in a white shirt and loose linen pants. "We'll ditch 'em." He winked at her. "Follow me."

He took her hand and led her along the corridors toward the east wing. "Aren't we heading right for them?"

"Yes, but they won't see us." He opened a door that she'd always assumed was some kind of closet, and stepped into the darkness. Her hand tingled in his as she stepped in after him. "Look out, there are some stairs." She followed him down, her heart pounding louder as they went farther down the strange staircase.

"Is there a light?" she whispered, wondering when the staircase would end.

"I don't think so." He squeezed her hand. "But we're nearly there."

"Where?"

AJ chuckled. "Nowhere."

The stairs ended, and stone clapped against the bottoms of her sandals. "What is this place?" Tiny points of light overhead—like cracks in the ceiling—illuminated a large room. The temperature was cool, a good twenty degrees lower than the midday warmth of the palace.

"Your guess is as good as mine. No one's used it in years. Vanu and I used to sneak out of the palace this way."

Cold fear trickled through her and she glanced over her shoulder. She could easily picture Vanu haunting a dim, subterranean space like this.

If he was even dead. The reporter's question from earlier nagged at her brain. Yes, it did unsettle her that they hadn't found a body. How could it not? Sometimes it seemed he was everywhere, his cold, wheedling voice in her head, criticizing everything she did.

She squeezed AJ's strong, warm hand. "Where does it bring you out?"

"You won't believe me if I tell you." Their shoes clicked along over the stone tiles as they headed farther and farther from the palace. The room narrowed again into a passageway, and Lani was alarmed by a roaring sound that grew louder as they walked.

She glanced up at AJ and saw his amused grin in the scant light from above. The thin strands of light became fainter until the corridor was almost pitch-black and the roar overhead boomed like the New York City subway. If AJ wasn't boldly leading the way, she'd have turned and run back to the palace long ago. They rounded a corner and a shaft of golden light broke through the chink between two doors. AJ pushed the doors open and led them out into blinding sun.

As her eyes adjusted, Lani realized the roar of sound was the crashing of a waterfall. They now stood directly behind the flow of water as it cascaded down the hillside.

Lani stared at the wall of water. Tiny droplets splashed her face and arms. "It's beautiful." She had to shout to make herself heard. "I've only ever seen it from above."

"Let's go somewhere quieter," murmured AJ in her ear. His hot breath on her skin made her shiver. Still holding her hand, he led her along a ledge of rock only a foot wide, then down a vine-covered hillside. The quiet rustle of the forest gradually replaced the rush of water over rock.

"Now I can breathe." AJ stretched and turned his face to the sun, which shone down through the trees. "I don't like living in a fishbowl."

"I'd think you'd be used to it, living in L.A."

"There you expect it when you're out and about, but they don't follow me home. I'm not that interesting." He grinned.

"You're apparently interesting enough to justify big travel budgets for all those journalists."

"It's not every day a B-movie director becomes king." He lifted his hand and stroked her cheek. The soft touch of his thumb made her shiver with pleasure. "And marries his brother's wife."

She tensed at his words. "And they don't even know about the baby. That would be quite a story."

"One more reason to keep it our secret. Everyone should be allowed some secrets." His fingers trailed down her back and his face hovered close. The scent of his skin, masculine and seductive, filled her senses. His lips met hers slowly, a soft collision, then they melted together.

Heat flooded through her as the kiss deepened. Her hands fisted in the soft cotton of AJ's shirt. She probably shouldn't be feeling desire, given the strange circumstances, but it pounded through her like a drum. Maybe all the years of pent-up longing, all the rejections and slights and hurts of her first marriage, had left her with a deep hunger.

She pressed herself against AJ, feeling her body mold to his hard chest. He groaned and his hands roamed down to cup her backside. He grew hard against her as arousal leaped between them like electric current.

"I am very attracted to you," she whispered when their lips pulled apart.

AJ laughed. "I can tell." He pressed another kiss to her moist lips. "And I like it when you're really hot for me, not just trying to push me into bed to carry out a complicated plan."

Lani blushed. "I'm so sorry."

"Don't be. This is making up for it." Her nipple thickened under his palm. "Come a bit farther into the jungle. If things haven't changed too much, there's a peaceful spot I remember."

He led her through a semi-tangle of vines and spiky palms until they reached a huge fig tree. Its enormous violin-shaped leaves shaded out the hot sun; underneath them grew a lush carpet of soft moss dotted with tiny white flowers. AJ gestured for her to sit down.

She lowered herself onto the cushioned surface and AJ joined her. "What a perfect place." Gnarled branches curved over them like protective arms.

"I used to sneak off and come here. I'd sit up in the tree, tucked away behind the leaves. No one ever found my hiding place." He nibbled her earlobe softly. Lani almost jumped at the sensation of his hot breath on her ear. "But I think I've found a hot spot on you."

She giggled. Then gasped when he did it again. Little flashes of sensation darted through her body. "How did you do that?"

"You mean this?" He trailed the tip of his tongue

along her neck, just below her ear. She shuddered at the sudden surge of heat deep in her belly.

"That, too," she breathed. "What's going on?"

A grin spread across AJ's sensual mouth. "It's called arousal." His brow furrowed. "This is new to you?"

"Completely." She'd never known anything like the pulsing heat that pounded in unexpected parts of her. He must be surprised that a married woman would be so…ignorant. "It wasn't like that before. It was very… official." She swallowed. What an odd way to describe her own sex life. Still, better than the truth—that it was virtually nonexistent and that "perfunctory" might be a better description. Vanu had never spent a single second touching her body just for pleasure.

Her train of thought went off the rails as AJ's hot mouth tracked down her neck. She writhed against him, enjoying the strange feelings that trickled right to her toes. He'd unbuttoned the back of her dress and now slid his hands inside it. When his fingertips touched her belly, her muscles contracted, making her buck against him.

"You're very sensitive." His deep chuckle rumbled against her skin. "Very responsive." Still behind her, he pushed her dress over her shoulders and it fell to her hips. He plucked at the thick embroidered sash that wrapped around her waist as part of the ceremonial dress for the press shoot—and served to hide her pregnancy. The silken folds pulled away and her dress fell about her thighs.

"How thoughtful of you to bring a blanket," murmured AJ. He spread the pretty blue and yellow cloth on the soft moss in front of them. "Our national dress does have its benefits. And here I was thinking it outdated and silly."

Lani laughed. "I guess the ancestors knew more than we realize." She lay on the silky fabric, stretching herself out in the dappled shade of the tree. Oddly, she didn't feel at all self-conscious, or even particularly naked. There was something accepting and easy about AJ that made her feel comfortable with him.

If she could be considered "comfortable" with so many different sensations and emotions pulsing and leaping through her body.

AJ's fingertips trailed along the inside of her thigh, stirring little rivulets of excitement beneath her skin. She let out a ragged sigh, which AJ met with a mischievous grin.

Suddenly she wanted to feel his body with her fingers. She unbuttoned his shirt and slid her hand inside. His skin was hot, the muscle hard and unyielding. She dragged her fingernails gently over his chest, down toward his waist. AJ flinched, his eyes half-closed, as she drew near the button on his pants. A smile crept across her mouth as she saw the evidence of his arousal pressing against his zipper. She let her fingers wander lower until her knuckles brushed his erection.

Judging from his languorous smile, AJ enjoyed her attentions. Encouraged by his sultry stare, she unbuttoned and unzipped his pants. They stripped off his clothes and underwear together, until they both lay naked on the embroidered blanket of Lani's colorful sash.

Shimmering droplets of sunlight snuck through the canopy to paint warm patterns on their skin. The peculiar fragrance of the jungle—thick, rich and almost honeyed—mingled with AJ's raw, masculine scent to create an intoxicating cocktail of arousal.

His thickly muscled body was a feast for the eyes. Lani eased herself closer to him until their chests bumped gently, then she let her fingers caress the rough skin of his thighs and the flat expanse of his belly. A mix of excitement, exhilaration and embarrassment stung her fingertips every time she drew near his erection. When at last she plucked up the courage to touch him, and to enjoy the feel of all that rigid passion in her hand, she almost cried out with relief.

Her fingertips vibrated with excitement as she let them explore the long, hard shape, and she drew in a long breath. She'd never actually touched that body part before. Vanu would never have given her the chance to play with him.

AJ leaned in and whispered, "I'm not even inside you yet and you're already breathless."

"Look who's talking," she teased. He jumped and jerked under her touch, muscles flexing as she caressed his skin. Desire rolled between them like a jungle mist, licking their skin and heating their blood.

On the one hand, Lani craved the feeling of him inside her. On the other, she loved the anticipation, the tension of the wait. She stroked his inner thigh with her forefinger and enjoyed the ragged groan that slipped from his chest. "You're killing me."

"But softly," she whispered, breathing her words into the hot skin of his neck before nibbling his ear the way he'd done with hers. His tortured response only heightened her pleasure. His skin tasted salty and delicious, and she let her tongue explore the chiseled line of his jaw, then probe between his lips.

Their kiss grew deep as they pressed their bodies together. AJ's hardness jutted into Lani's side and for a second she felt a twinge of apprehension. He was so…

big. So unlike Vanu. What if she couldn't handle him? What if it hurt?

"What is going through your mind?"

She cracked open her eyes to find AJ's fixed on her. An expression of amusement brightened his face.

"Uh, nothing."

"That's what I'd hoped for, but expressions keep fluttering across your face like a flock of birds."

"I guess I'm just nervous." She bit her lip. "I'm not… experienced. I don't want to let you down."

"Let me down?" AJ laughed. "About the only way you could do that is by standing up and getting dressed. Now stop worrying." He feigned a stern frown. "In fact, I'm going to do my best to wipe all thoughts from your mind."

In an instant his mouth was between her legs. Lani gasped with shock as he sucked—quite hard— and caused her body to jerk as a sweet, sharp thrill ricocheted through her. He flicked his tongue back and forth over her sensitive spot, which made her muscles convulse and twitch in a way that was downright alarming. She writhed on the soft fabric of her sash, grasping first at the silky fabric and the ground beneath, then at AJ's head and shoulders as he drove her further and further into a mysterious world of intense sensation and shocking pleasure.

She cried out as a fierce ripple of sensation jolted her. Waves of heat rolled through her, emerging from her mouth as moans. She realized her fingers were fisted in his thick hair, and she pulled them loose, then groped for him as another alarming tidal wave surged through her.

AJ's hands roamed over her, stroking her waist and breasts as he rose up to meet her. Her eyes opened to see his dark gaze blazing just over hers. "Much better." His wicked grin only stirred the fevered passion pounding through her.

"Enter me, please." She craved him inside her, ached for him.

He chuckled. "You make yourself sound like Aladdin's cave." His words rasped hotly at her neck as he lowered himself over her. "I can't wait to come in, but I don't know the magic word."

Quivering with excitement, Lani lifted herself to meet him. "Please."

"That's an easy one to remember." He layered hot kisses on her face and neck. "Please may I come in?"

"Yes, yes," Lani gasped, almost shouting at the way he tortured her. She tilted her hips to him, begging with her body. She could feel his heartbeat through his skin, strong and insistent, like her own. His musky, male scent only added to her torment. She could tell he was every bit as aroused as she. Was he going to torture her forever?

He entered her very, very slowly. First with his fingers, probing her slick depths. When he decided she was ready—and oh, was she ready—he probed her with the tip of his member. A tiny cry fled her lips as anticipation got the better of her.

She pushed her fingers into his back, unconsciously urging him on. Warmth and pleasure filled her as he slid inside her and his chest lowered over hers. His throaty moan filled her ear as he started to move. She arched against him, taking him deeper, welcoming him into her body and into her life.

I love you. She got an urge to say it, but something held her back.

It was too soon for love; the circumstances were

too strange and pressured. She didn't want to seem too demanding, as if she expected him to love her back.

And maybe it was just sheer madness, the delicious thrills cascading through her as AJ moved inside her.

AJ pulled her upright until they were in a sitting position, legs interlaced, facing each other, with him still buried deep. A perfect position for kissing.

AJ licked her lips, and she returned the gesture, tasting his smile, then enjoying the slight roughness of his cheeks. She could feel him inside her, slight movements, subtle throbs, letting her feel his arousal and the deep connection between them.

When kissing—and barely moving—threatened to drive her completely over the edge, AJ lay back until she was sitting on top of him. Alarm flashed through her. She was supposed to be in control, and she had no idea what to do.

"Anything," he murmured, as if in answer to her question. "Whatever feels good."

She trailed her finger along the middle of his chest, eyes half-open to enjoy the view. She wriggled a little, and felt him move inside her. A smile spread across her face and his at the same time. "This definitely feels good."

Eyes closed again, she gently rocked back and forth, amazed at the new points of pleasure this position awakened. She found herself moving faster and higher, experimenting with rhythms to take herself right to the next peak, and then pulling back. Beneath her, AJ groaned, his hands stroking her skin, teasing her.

"Let go," AJ urged her.

Could she? Something inside her kept holding her back. She'd never experienced this kind of arousal before. She could tell she was close to the brink of something big, and it scared her.

"It'll feel good, I promise." AJ's soft voice penetrated her thoughts.

Living at the palace she'd grown used to being "on duty" all the time. Always polite and prepared and ready for anything—even the worst Vanu could dish out. "Letting go" was no longer in her vocabulary. She had been too busy shoring herself up.

A bird chirped overhead and a warm breeze caressed her skin. She'd almost forgotten they were deep in the jungle. Apparently she'd let go quite a lot already!

She quickened the pace, and AJ encouraged her with his roving hands. Hot spots of excitement seemed to become even more sensitive and the tension inside her built and grew until she felt white-hot all over.

Something in her brain told her to slow down, but her body urged her to keep going—and she obeyed, moving with more and more urgency until suddenly everything seemed to explode into a million pieces, showering stars down over them where they lay on the jungle floor.

She collapsed onto the solid expanse of AJ's chest. His breathing labored, he wrapped his arms around her and held her in his soft embrace while the shower of stars gradually drifted down and settled around them, leaving her tingling and warm in all sorts of unexpected places.

"See what I mean?" AJ said after a while.

She nodded, not quite able to form words. She'd never imagined that sex could be like that. Her previous experiences had been so stilted, so fraught with tension, that she honestly hadn't enjoyed them at all—though she'd certainly pretended to. Vanu had made no such pretense.

With AJ everything was completely, utterly and gloriously different. At least she thought it was. "Did you enjoy it, too?" Her voice sounded a little shaky.

AJ's chest rumbled with laughter. "What do you think?" His dark eyes glittered with humor.

"I don't seem to be able to think at all right now."

"Good."

AJ loved the feel of her in his arms. Completely relaxed, Lani sprawled over him like he was a giant mattress. It was intriguing that such a fiery vixen lived beneath that placid exterior. Well, he might have guessed, after the way she practically kissed his face off that first time.

"What are you laughing about?" Her voice tinkled in his ear. She sounded happy, which filled him with joy.

"At how my life is filled with surprises. In a good way." He stroked her hair.

Who'd have ever imagined him planning to settle back in Rahiri? In truth, Vanu had been the reason he'd left. The future king, Vanu had been cherished and encouraged and adored. Intelligent and charming when he wanted to be, he'd wrapped his parents around his long and surprisingly strong fingers.

AJ could remember the cruel grip of those fingers all too well, though often as not Vanu used words with more brutal force. He employed his considerable genius in coming up with ways to make AJ look guilty of something, meaning that AJ was nearly always in trouble, even when he did manage to keep a lid on his admittedly rambunctious nature.

But now Vanu was gone. And with the happy result that he'd left a lovely wife in dire need of a new husband. Vanu must have turned on the charm with Lani. She had probably never gotten a glimpse of his dark side. Why spoil her memories? He decided to keep his to himself.

"Only seven months until our baby arrives." He spoke softly, stroking Lani's cheek.

She started slightly. "It seems so soon."

"Tell me about it." He was still trying to wrap his mind around the idea of being a father. He'd decided that the baby would be his in every way. Well, every way that mattered, and that's how he intended to approach the situation. "Do you have a nickname for him or her already? One of my producers used to call hers Jellybean while she was pregnant."

Lani laughed. "I don't. I guess I should come up with something." She gazed skyward for a minute, her golden eyes thoughtful. "Puaiti."

"Little flower. But what if it's a boy?"

"Why can't a boy be a flower, too?" She raised a slim brow.

"Good point. Why should girls get all the nice-smelling pretty stuff? How's little Puaiti feeling?"

Lani closed her eyes for a minute and rested her fingers on her stomach, as if listening. "I'm not hearing any complaints."

"Do you feel any kicking yet?"

"No. I don't think that happens for a few more weeks. I don't really feel different at all. Well, except when I feel ill." She paused and looked right at him. "You know something? Ever since I told you about the baby, I haven't felt ill at all."

"Maybe Puaiti realized she'd have to make you sick or you wouldn't realize she was there."

"Quite possible. And she'd have been right." She frowned. "But why are you calling Puaiti a she? She could be a he."

He shrugged. "We'll just have to use both."

"Would you like to find out the gender before the birth?"

AJ stroked Lani's cheek. "I don't know that I would. I'm getting used to being surprised, and I find I like it. Do you have a preference for a girl or boy?"

Lani shook her head. A sweet smile played about her lips. "Either will be wonderful. I've wanted a child for so long, and your mom is going to love having a grandchild to spoil."

A crashing sound in the undergrowth nearby made them sit up. "What was that?" AJ peered through the leaves. He'd been gone a long time, but he didn't remember any forest animals big enough to make that much sound.

"I don't know." Lani grabbed her dress. "We'd better get dressed."

AJ tugged his shirt and pants on, then helped rewind Lani's rather wrinkled sash around her still-slim waist. He continued to hear a rustling sound in the distance.

"Was that a voice?" whispered Lani, eyes wide with alarm.

AJ strained his ears. It was hard to distinguish sounds above the low hum of the jungle, all the insects and birds and the rustling leaves. Then again, he did hear a voice. "It's a man. Speaking English." Why would someone be way out here? "Maybe the journalists have started wandering about looking for scandal."

"If they find us they might well have it." Lani smoothed her dress with anxious fingers. "We're not married yet."

"We'd better head back to the passageway." He took Lani's hand and led her back up toward the waterfall. He didn't want her being harassed by some bozo out for a picture and quick buck.

They set off up a steep hill. At the top, he heard the voice again, and turned to peer through the trees. It was impossible to see anyone through the dense leaf canopy, but then he heard quite clearly: "They say he went out late at night on a boat."

AJ froze. The were talking about Vanu. Could they be looking for the body?

Lani didn't seem to have heard. She was distracted, adjusting her sandal.

"But what if he didn't get on a boat? What if he came out here and got lost?"

An icy finger of dread slid down AJ's back. He didn't want Lani to get wind of their idle speculation. "Are you okay?"

"Great." She smiled brightly. He led her farther up the hill until the roar of water cloaked out all other sounds. Still, an odd sense of unease nagged at him. Suddenly all these curious strangers were trudging through their jungles and making footprints on the beaches. What if they did find something?

And what if it was something none of them expected at all?

Seven

"Thank heavens you're back!" Priia stood up from the plush armchair surrounded by her embroidery tools. Servants had whisked AJ and Lani to her study as soon as the girl became spotted back in the palace hallways. The servants slipped out, closing the door behind them.

AJ's heart thumped. Something was wrong but no one would tell him what. "What's going on?"

"We just got a phone call that a reporter found Vanu's boat."

Lani froze. "Where is it?"

Priia dabbed at her eyes with an already moist handkerchief. "On the tiny atoll to the northwest. The one they call Egg Island."

AJ shoved a hand through his hair. "Did they find Vanu?"

His mom shook her head. "So far there's been no sign of him."

AJ shot a glance at Lani. Her hands were trembling and one of them flew to her mouth.

"So he could be alive." AJ managed to force out the words.

"Yes. It's possible." Priia sniffed. "The atoll is small but very densely wooded. There's plenty of food there for someone to survive."

Dread crawled over AJ like a poisonous spider. Could Vanu be hidden somewhere in the forest?

Lani had begun to weep. Probably with joy that her once-dead husband might still be alive. AJ sucked in a ragged breath as a bitter taste filled his mouth. "We need to send out a search party."

"They're getting ready to leave. The fire department and the lifeboat service are all involved. And of course the journalists." She pressed her handkerchief to her face. "It seems too much to hope for, but maybe he's about to come back to us."

Lani approached Priia and put her arms around her. AJ's heart swelled at her generous gesture. Caring and thoughtful as well as lovely, Lani was far too good to be wasted on Vanu. Anger roiled in his chest along with savage jealously. Could Vanu return from the grave and snatch Lani from his arms?

Yes. That was exactly the kind of party trick Vanu would take great pleasure in.

"Didn't they search Egg Island when he disappeared?" He couldn't understand how Vanu's boat could appear like a horrible vision after all this time.

Priia looked up. "It's a dense forest, with many natural caves. The boat had drifted into a cavern that's hidden at high tide." She let out a sob. "It will be hard to find him if he's still alive, but we must keep positive."

A knock on the door startled them all. "Come in," said Priia, shakily.

The head footman entered, head slightly bowed. "The reporters, they're anxious for a statement."

"Oh, goodness." Priia waved her handkerchief. "AJ, could you go tell them something?"

"Like what? We don't know any more than they do. Less, probably."

The head footman seemed to shrink a bit, and stared at the floor. "They want to know how this affects the wedding plans."

Lani let out a little gasp, then hid her face.

The dark reality of the situation settled over AJ like an executioner's hood. "It's off. Lani can't consider remarrying while her husband might be alive." His words came out cold and hard.

And what about the baby he'd grown to think of as his? Vanu would claim the child as well. It was his, after all, just like Lani.

AJ suppressed a curse. Only a brief while ago he and Lani had lain, wrapped in each other, surrounded by the warm embrace of the jungle, looking forward to a joyous future together with their new family.

Now he saw that future evaporating like a jungle mist.

"Did they find any signs that he survived?" AJ questioned the footman.

"They found footprints leading up out of the cave. So it seems he did walk away from it."

Lani whimpered and tears rolled down her cheeks. AJ tried to suppress the ugly surge of anger that rose in him at the sight. She was obviously distressed and hopeful that Vanu was still alive.

Yes, it hurt. Especially since he'd felt a deep connection with her during their lovemaking. Of course that was probably his body talking rather than his brain. "I'll go join the search party. Just stay away from the press until we know more." He turned and marched from the room, unable to even look at Lani.

AJ cursed himself for being drawn into this nightmare. How had he gone from wanting to leave at the earliest opportunity to hating the fact that he'd *have* to leave?

He returned late at night, sticky and tired from combing through the jungle. It probably hadn't done his soul much good that he was hoping against hope that they'd find a body, not a live Vanu with an ugly smirk on his face. As it turned out, they'd found nothing at all and the search was scheduled to resume the following morning.

No one spoke much at dinner, and Priia retired early, begging a headache.

Lani seemed very tense, avoiding his gaze. No doubt she felt guilty that she'd made love to another man while her husband might still be alive.

"It's not your fault," he murmured. "You had no idea he might still be out there."

"I know." She didn't meet his gaze. "No one could have known."

"The fire chief thinks he's alive." He studied her face. A muscle spasmed in her cheek. "They found traces of a fire in another natural cave. Looks like someone stayed there."

"That's wonderful." Lani's voice sounded oddly hollow. "It would be such a miracle for him to survive for so long by himself."

"He never was the rugged, outdoors type." AJ frowned.

It was hard to imagine Vanu picking a berry to feed himself, let alone lighting a fire. He'd required a large staff just to get dressed in the morning. "But I suppose anything is possible. People can act differently in a life-or-death situation."

"Yes." Lani sat ramrod straight. Unapproachable. Not that he'd even think of trying to touch her now. How odd, when he'd enjoyed touching almost every inch of her luscious body only hours earlier.

His life seemed to be spinning like a weather vane in the wind lately. He'd had calls from L.A. this afternoon asking if—due to the shift in circumstance—he'd be back to oversee the edits for *Hellcat*. He'd replied honestly: that he had no idea.

The dim light in the dining room picked out the gold threaded through Lani's lustrous hair. Soon, perhaps Vanu would be running his bony fingers through it again. AJ fought a wave of revulsion. "How are you feeling? I'm sure the stress must be hard on you when you're pregnant."

"I'm okay." She shot him a wary glance with those wide, honey-colored eyes.

He cursed the surge of lust that jolted through him. "Must be a little odd to be dangling between two men like this." His words sounded cruel, and maybe that's what he intended. Pain tightened his muscles and hardened his heart.

Lani shuddered and a small sob escaped her mouth. "It's terrible."

AJ's hands itched to reach out and touch hers. But that would only deepen his torment. "No one will ever know what happened between us today. It'll be yet another secret we'll keep forever."

Lani nodded. Tears glittered in her eyes. "Yes. I won't tell anyone. Especially Vanu."

AJ's flesh crawled at the thought of her talking to Vanu again, sharing intimacies. In such a short time he'd developed powerful feelings for Lani. He'd never felt anything like them before in all his years of adventures with the fairer sex.

And the child. His initial revulsion at the deception had quickly transformed into a firm conviction that he could raise this child and love it as his own. He'd been prepared to lie and pretend and carry out a charade to everyone else's fantasy of the perfect royal family come true.

He glanced up and saw Lani's delicate profile turned to look out the window. Just yesterday his bold and tender new feelings had been convenient rather than crazy. Now they were disastrous. He had to comfort and support the woman he craved as she hoped and prayed for the safe return of her husband.

Pain crashed over him in an untidy wave. He staggered to his feet and sucked in a breath of moist night air.

He'd spent his childhood in his brother's shadow, and now it stretched out from the grave to cast him into darkness once again.

Lani didn't love him. Didn't have any feelings for him other than a sense of duty and some rather unexpected lust. He'd been fool enough to mistake that for far more.

He'd never let himself make that mistake again.

Lani paced back and forth in her room all morning. The crews were out for the second day, combing through the jungle on the uninhabited atoll.

She hated the way they described it as "searching for Vanu," as if they'd find him there, perhaps lazing on a sandy beach, waiting for them to take him home. No one said anything as grim as "hoping to recover a body." Priia wouldn't hear any of that. As far as she was concerned, he was alive and well and on his way home.

And Lani knew she was probably cursed to eternal damnation for hoping otherwise.

How could she wish someone dead? Only a truly evil person would have a thought like that. Obviously she wasn't the "nice" girl AJ had originally mistaken her for. She'd certainly jumped on him with reckless abandon, and she couldn't even blame it on "duty" anymore. She'd made no effort to hide her lusty enjoyment of AJ's body.

She blew out hard. Everything had been so perfect for those few brief hours. Now she was back, snared in the web of pretense and pain that had been her marriage to Vanu. Pretending to be happy—or at least content— while inside she was longing for freedom.

A knock on the door startled her.

"Dinner is ready." The shy girl servant darted in and out like a lizard. No one would look her in the eye since Vanu's boat was found. They'd all been so thrilled about the plans for the wedding and AJ's return to Rahiri, and now they were supposed to be overjoyed about Vanu's possible survival.

No one knew what to think or how to behave. Least of all Lani. AJ was giving her the cold shoulder, too. She understood that he was in an awkward situation, but it was upsetting to suddenly feel as if she couldn't talk to him.

She wandered along the hallway slowly, not looking

forward to the meal. Terrified of any further news of Vanu's miraculous survival.

When she arrived in the dining room, she saw Priia sitting in her usual chair, sobbing, while AJ wrapped his arms around her.

All the servants hung their heads and ducked their gazes as she passed.

"They found his body." AJ looked up and mouthed the words softly, then tugged his gaze away immediately.

Relief welled inside her like a flood. "Oh, no," she managed, trying to sound upset. Her hands started shaking and her heart pounded. She wanted to jump up and down or shout because she'd been so afraid of being Vanu's plaything again. Happy tears sprang to her eyes and she let them roll down her cheeks.

She resisted a sharp urge to ask for details to make his death real, but managed to restrain herself. What did it matter how he died, as long as he was really gone for good.

AJ looked up at her tears, then glanced away. Priia's sobbing was merciless, inconsolable, as it had been in those first days and nights after Vanu disappeared.

"I'm so sorry, Mama," whispered Lani. She stroked Priia's hand. "It was too much of a miracle to hope for." Her own tears splashed into her mother-in-law's lap and mingled with Priia's, despite their very different motivations.

"At least we'll have his child," rasped Priia. Lani's eyes widened. Apparently in her grief she was forgetting that no one knew about the pregnancy. She glanced around. The servants had tactfully left the room. Still...

AJ's brow was lowered and his expression dark. He wouldn't meet her gaze.

"The child will give us something to live for," continued Priia, through her sobs. "It does seem cruel that we have to go through mourning him again. I was finally coming to terms with his loss, and now..." Her shoulders shook.

Lani squeezed her hand. "We'll just have to go on as best we can."

"I've got some phone calls to make." AJ's voice was gruff. Lani looked up, startled, as he strode from the room. She wanted to run after him, to ask him for details about Vanu's death—perhaps to reassure herself that this time he really was dead.

She also wanted reassurance that everything was still okay between them.

Her stomach contracted and a wave of nausea rose through her. Her first in several days. She had a grim feeling that everything had changed between her and AJ. That Vanu's unexpected reappearance, even in death, had somehow ruined everything.

AJ stormed along the palace corridor, blood pounding in his brain. How had he ever thought this could work? Had he really believed he could step into Vanu's shoes—precious Vanu, the beloved eldest son who could do no wrong—and take over?

Ridiculous. He must have been totally addled by lust. It was hard to blame himself because, after all, Lani was undeniably one of the most beautiful women on earth. He'd let desire interfere with his common sense and even convinced himself that she had feelings for him.

But of course she hadn't fallen madly in love with

him right after her husband's death. She was still in shock, especially with the pregnancy messing up her hormones. He'd come on way too strong and she'd reacted as she felt she was supposed to. Just trying to be a "nice Rahiian maiden," when all along she was carrying a torch for Vanu.

He shoved into his room. The room he'd spent his childhood in and been glad to leave. Which seemed ungrateful, since not many people would complain about spacious chambers in a royal palace. But they'd felt like a prison to him once, and now the decorative carvings started to look like bars again. He'd almost— almost—been trapped into living someone else's life.

He picked up the phone and pushed the third button on his speed dial. His producer, Jerry. When Jerry answered he didn't mince words. "I'll be back tomorrow. Sooner if I can get a flight."

"But I thought your brother turned up dead."

"He did."

"Sorry, I didn't mean to say that so crudely. I'm sorry for your loss."

"I know. It's okay." Being honest that you were glad someone was dead was one of the last taboos left.

"Doesn't that mean that you need to take over?"

"You can't take over from a living god, and I'm not going to walk in his shadow the rest of my life. I've got a good life in L.A. and I'm coming back to it."

"Isn't there some tradition that you have to marry your brother's wife?" Jerry's tone didn't hide his curiosity—the same kind of prurient interest that had sent the media chasing down to Rahiri to ogle them.

"There was, but I'm breaking with it. Why should she be forced into marrying someone she doesn't care about?" Not to mention giving her late husband's baby to him to raise. His chest tightened.

"That is a bit heavy. Still, you two looked good together on *Entertainment Tonight*."

"Jerry, you and I know better than anyone how easy it is to create an illusion with a camera."

"Too true. Well, if you're ready, we'll soon be right back at it. Give me a call when you hit town and we'll hash through some details."

"Perfect."

AJ put down the phone, a mixture of conviction and regret mingling in his heart. What a vivid fantasy it had been, for a few brief days. King AJ and his lovely family, ruling the island paradise he'd finally come home to.

Way too sappy to put in a movie, so why would he think it could happen in real life?

He jerked open the closet door and grabbed an armful of clothes off the rack. Shoved them right into his suitcase. He didn't need servants to fold and fluff everything for him. He'd gotten along just fine without them for over a decade and he was damned if he'd turn into a spoiled fop like Vanu.

He went into the bathroom and swiped his toiletries off the marble shelf and into a plastic bag. A scan of the room confirmed that he'd removed all traces of his brief presence.

Now to confront Lani.

His chest ached. He'd so much rather have slipped away without seeing her again. Experience had proved he didn't have much self-control around her. Getting to know her hadn't helped, either. Did he really have to find out that she was warm and thoughtful as well as gorgeous? It would have been better if he'd left right after the funeral.

He would have preferred as well not to know how responsive and exciting she was during sex. If that's how she performed with a man she was being forced to marry while still mourning her husband, imagine what she'd be like if she was really in love?

Don't. There was no point in thinking about what-ifs. He was not going to participate in this arranged marriage charade any longer.

He zipped up his suitcase and pulled out the handle. Soon he'd be marching along the corridors at LAX, a free man again.

Finding Lani wasn't easy. He walked all over the palace, asking everyone he met for almost an hour, tension building in his muscles, before he finally tracked her down on a stone bench by a reflecting pool in the garden.

She glanced up, startled, as he approached.

"Don't worry. I'm not staying." He almost growled the words, then regretted his hostile tone. This whole mess wasn't really her fault. She'd been bullied into it, the same way he had.

He glanced at the round pool, where reflected leaves danced across its shimmering surface, hiding its depths from view. "You'll be a good queen until the baby comes of age. The elders are wise and thoughtful and really don't need any help to run the country, though I'm sure they'll welcome new ideas about education and—"

"You're not really leaving." Her eyes widened.

"I really am. Booked on tonight's flight. Back on the course I should have stuck with from day one." Before he'd become intrigued, then utterly seduced, by her.

Her face totally still, she stared at him, apparently lost for words. And why should she have to come up with words? They were all tired of saying things they didn't mean. She that she was thrilled to be marrying a total stranger, he that he was so sad his rotten older brother was dead. Enough with the pretense.

"It'll be hard on Mom. That's the one part I really regret."

Lani blinked. He saw her shoulders stiffen. "Yes. But why are you leaving? Is it because of me?" Her lips tightened.

"It's not because of you." He shoved a hand through his hair. He owed her his honesty after all they'd been through over the last few days. "If anything, you're the reason I almost made the wrong decision to stay. You're a good person, Lani, as well as a very beautiful one. But you're my brother's wife, not mine. I can't step into his life and walk in his footsteps. I have my own life that I made for myself, and that's where I need to be."

"Everyone wants you to stay." Her voice was oddly hollow.

AJ straightened his back. "Everyone? I doubt it. I don't think people pay much more attention to who's in the palace than to who's on *Instant Millionaire* every Wednesday. I'm going to make an announcement to the media so there won't be any guessing and suspense."

"Have you told Priia yet?" Lani twisted her hands into her skirt.

AJ's stomach clenched. "I'm going to tell her now, and I know it won't be easy."

"She'll be devastated."

"I know, but it can't be helped." Better than entering into a marriage with a woman who hadn't chosen him, and who'd never stop being his brother's wife.

Lani looked down at her lap, avoiding his glance. Maybe she resented the fact that he'd decided to put emotion before duty. After all, she'd demonstrated her readiness to sacrifice everything for the good of Rahiri.

He wasn't made of such stern stuff.

And he really did want her to be happy. "I hope the rest of your pregnancy goes smoothly." His voice softened. "And that the birth is uneventful. You'll be able to tell everyone that it's Vanu's baby now. No more living a lie."

Lani swallowed. "Yes. I suppose that's good." Her voice sounded flat. "Things did get awfully complicated."

"Which should have been the first clue we were heading in the wrong direction." His fingers itched to touch her, just one last time. To feel her soft skin beneath his palm and inhale her delicate floral scent.

But he resisted. "Goodbye, Lani."

"Goodbye, AJ." She looked up at last, wide eyes brimming with tears. "Good luck to you. I hope everything works out the way you want it to."

He frowned. "Thanks. And for you and the baby, too. I'm sure I'll be in touch after things settle down a bit."

She nodded, lips pressed together. She hadn't risen from the bench. Just sat there like a lovely statue, fingers twisted into the silk of her dress.

He spun on his heel and marched away before he could do anything stupid.

Lani slumped on the bench as he walked away. She didn't even have the urge to run after him. It seemed normal, natural, that she should be left here alone and loveless while he went back to his life in L.A. Isn't that just what she'd expected, after all?

He'd been swept along on the tide of excitement that they'd mistaken for destiny—all the pomp of the funeral and Priia's festive gathering—and he'd gotten temporarily sidetracked into thinking he'd like to return to Rahiri.

Vanu's unwitting intervention had woken him up.

Trust Vanu to ruin everything.

The reappearance of his boat and the resulting hitch in their plans had given AJ time to realize he didn't want the life Priia had plotted out for him—or her.

It hurt—really hurt.

She pressed her fingers gently into her belly and tried to ignore the hollow space that seemed to be opening up inside her. At least she had the baby to look forward to, and AJ was right, the elders could rule the country without any help from the palace. They'd certainly been doing it while Vanu was king, as he'd taken zero interest in the country's affairs. Rahiri would be fine.

But would she?

It didn't seem fair to taste happiness like that, then have it rudely snatched away.

At first she'd been wary of AJ, and hoped he'd leave. But now that she'd gotten to know him, she wanted desperately for him to stay. He'd looked genuinely excited about raising the baby with her. She'd been so sure that—at last—everything was going to work out for the best. That she'd finally get to be happy.

But that had been too much to hope for.

A few weeks ago she'd have been pleased to be left quietly alone. She hadn't known about the baby then, but she'd at least been relieved to be rid of Vanu. Now she craved the family she'd always wanted as a child.

A mother and father together, as hers had been when she was little, before their marriage broke up and she and her mother came back to Rahiri.

She let out a deep sigh, picked up a small stone and tossed it into the pool. A splash radiated out into huge ripples that filled the round surface and lapped against the walls. AJ's arrival had changed everything, even her dreams.

She no longer wanted to be left quietly alone, merely to live out her days without having to endure cruel treatment from a man she despised. Now she wanted so much more: affection, conversation, humor and, of course, the dangerous and delicious passion that AJ had awakened in her.

But AJ didn't want to share it with her. He'd chosen to return to his life in L.A. and the freedom that came with it. He wouldn't be tied down by responsibilities to a nation, or a woman.

Sadness soaked through her. Probably right now AJ was telling the reporters who never left the palace of his plans to abandon Rahiri—and her. In a short while she'd be paraded in front of them to embrace her new, solitary role as queen, and to announce the pregnancy.

And she'd do it all alone. Not physically alone, with her doting mother-in-law and the palace staff all around her, but in the ways that were important, the empty, hungry places in her heart, she'd be alone.

"We must stop him!" Priia's voice rang out into the garden from the nearby sitting room. "I told him he can't go. It's impossible!"

"We can't stop him," Lani mouthed back in barely a whisper.

Her mother-in-law ran out into the garden and

grabbed her arms. "AJ's heading for the airport." Her long nails cut into Lani's skin. "He can't leave us. We need him."

"I know we want him here." Lani rose and spoke softly. "But he needs to leave and we have to let him."

Priia's eyes were still wide with shock. "I could call the airport and tell them to ground the plane."

Lani shook her head. "You can't keep him here by force. It has to be his choice."

"But he chose to stay. He announced to all of us at the banquet that he…" The first tear rolled from Priia's dark eyes.

You pressured him into it, Lani wanted to say. But she held her tongue. No need to pour salt on Priia's already sore wounds. But this was exactly why it was a bad idea to go after him now. Trying to force the issue hadn't helped at all. He was still leaving, and they were right back where they started.

Which wasn't such a bad place after all.

She drew in a steadying breath. "We'll be fine. The baby will be our next king or queen."

Priia looked up. "The baby, yes! Oh, sweetheart." She drew in a steadying breath. "And now I suppose we can tell people it's Vanu's child."

Lani looked down. "Yes, there's no reason not to."

Her mother-in-law dabbed at her eyes with one of her embroidered handkerchiefs. "It is a blessing having his baby to remember him by. And you can rule in the meantime. It's been a long time since Rahiri had a queen, because usually our people have so many boys ready to…"

Her voice trailed off, then she cleared her throat. "You're right, of course, my dear. We must meet every challenge life throws at us with our heads held high.

Thank the heavens for bringing you into our lives, sweet Lani. I don't know what I'd do without you."

They hugged and Lani did indeed feel a tiny bit reassured. She'd gotten along just fine without AJ around before, and she'd be a-okay without him again.

At least she hoped so.

Eight

AJ had hoped that media coverage of Rahiri would cease now there was no longer a Hollywood director involved. Apparently, though, he was not the main attraction. He'd been back in L.A. two months and stories continued daily on the splashy entertainment shows and in the celebrity press, and blogs buzzed with the latest tidbits and speculations from the palace.

He'd underestimated the hold Lani's beauty would have on the popular imagination. People couldn't seem to get enough of her stunning face, which could not take a bad photo. Her slightly exotic features and unique coloring entranced and intrigued people and made them want to know more about her and her fabulous royal existence.

Which didn't help, because AJ couldn't stop thinking about her, either.

He strode across his foyer and grabbed the newest

pile of mail off the hall table. He'd arranged for his clipping service to send him everything related to the palace, not because he felt personally involved, but so he'd at least know what was going on if someone asked.

He flipped through a thick file of fresh clippings, forcing himself not to linger on any pictures. There was one in particular they seemed to latch on to, a half profile shot that perfectly captured the adorable tilt of her nose and the sparkle in her golden eyes.

He knew what they'd cut out of the photo—him. She'd been gazing at him with that bright look on her face. Now he was the villain of the piece, the one who had let her down to pursue his big-deal career and go back to chasing designer miniskirts in L.A.

They were half-right, really.

But his dropping out of the picture had only seemed to intensify their interest in Lani and her predicament: the lovely princess, so recently widowed and now jilted by her presumed fiancé. Her pregnancy had hit the media like a neutron bomb. Poor lonely Lani, left to raise a child with no one to care for her.

Of course he knew better. She had a staff of nearly fifty and a mother-in-law who rarely gave her a moment's peace.

One story told of the hordes of men who'd submitted details and photos in the hope that she'd choose one of them to be her husband. He was pretty confident the applications were being shredded on arrival at the palace, but he couldn't help feeling a sting of envy.

Which was ridiculous, because eventually Lani would marry someone else.

He turned and strode back into the kitchen. His home used to seem so calm and uncluttered. Lately it just looked bleak. All the black and white furnishings looked garish and pretentious after the soft natural hues and hand-carved woods of the palace.

At least he was busy. Editing sessions on *Hellcat* stretched late into the night and he was already deep in pre-production on the next *Dragon Chaser* movie.

That meant he wouldn't have time to read all the blogs and websites his Google Alerts were picking up about Lani's upcoming coronation. Already he knew exactly what kind of dress she'd be wearing, and the ancient hammered-gold jewelry she'd put on and how her palms would be painted with berry juice and her skin brushed with golden pollen. He didn't know this because he'd grown up in the palace. He'd learned it all on *E!* along with everyone else.

An enterprising retailer in Beverly Hills had come out with a line of Rahiian dresses, woven from the rich silk of the island but cut to reveal a bit more gym-toned leg than the originals.

Twice he'd seen Lani paraded before the cameras with a tight smile on her lips. He could imagine his mom behind the scenes, urging her out there and telling her to put on her best face. But he could see past it. Her mouth might be forced into a cheerful grin, but the light in her eyes had dimmed noticeably.

Or did he imagine that? Maybe he just wanted her to be pale and pining since he'd gone. He'd already told them he wouldn't be there for the coronation. Let them sing Vanu's praises and exclaim over how AJ would never have made a good king, with his Hollywood decadence and fickle attitudes.

He didn't want to see Lani, either. Not so soon. He couldn't guarantee his immunity to her vibrant smile. Just a whiff of her scent might send him into a tailspin.

The taste of her was still too fresh on his lips, the pain of leaving her too raw in his heart.

It was for the best though. He wasn't Vanu and sure as heck didn't want to play second fiddle to his brother's memory for the rest of his life. Much better to move on and strike out for new frontiers.

Speaking of which, an old flame of his had left a message on his machine. A Danish beauty who'd had a small part in one of his early movies was back in town for a couple of weeks and wanted to get together. Probably just what he needed to pry his mind off Lani.

He reached for the phone and listened to the bubbly message again. Why not take her to the premiere of the new Spielberg movie that Friday? She was good company. Loved to dance, too. They could have some dinner, then go out to that new club everyone kept raving about.

But something kept his fingers from dialing her number.

He found himself wandering back into the kitchen, where the stack of clippings lay sprawled on the stone counter, that now-famous picture on the top. Lani's wide eyes, sparkling with what anyone might mistake for happiness, seemed to look right at him, just as they had when the picture was taken.

AJ drew in a deep breath. He'd get over her. Eventually. But until then it wasn't really fair to take out another girl. He'd only be looking at her and wishing he was with Lani.

Better to wait until time took the edge off a bit. Until he started to forget the soft touch of her fingers on his skin, and the sweet song of her laugh.

Of course, it would help if he could stop thinking about her for five solid minutes.

Lani lay awake in her bedroom, staring at the dark ceiling. Counting imaginary sheep didn't help. Counting live lizards didn't help, either. Even the baby seemed restless and unsettled. It was hard to sleep when something was eating at you.

She'd promised herself that she'd never tell anyone the truth about Vanu. That she'd keep up the pretense of a happy marriage and allow her mother-in-law to remember her eldest son as a paragon of virtue.

But something AJ had said made her think it was her silence on the subject that had driven him away. That he thought of her as Vanu's wife, and that he couldn't step into his brother's life and walk in his footsteps.

She hadn't really made the connection at the time, but lately the thought pestered her night and day: Would he feel differently if he knew that she hated Vanu and was secretly glad he was gone?

Such a blunt declaration would definitely bare the darkness in her soul, even if Vanu had put it there. AJ might despise her for her disloyalty, and if Priia ever found out—which she might, since AJ was not one to mince words—she'd be shocked and deeply hurt, as much by Lani's betrayal of Vanu as by the idea that her son was not the sweet boy she chose to remember.

Then there was the baby. Vanu's child. If she told people that Vanu was harsh and cold and unloving, would her child learn this about his or her own father?

Still…if she never told anyone, these thoughts might torment her and keep her awake at night for the rest of her life.

AJ had been gone for nearly a month—twenty-three days, to be precise—and she still ached for him. She hadn't seen or heard anything of him in all that time, except the secondhand report that he would not be coming to the coronation. But she could remember the feel of his body against hers as if he'd just left the room. Alone at night, she imagined his hot breath on her skin and heard his voice soft in her ear.

If she phoned him, she really could hear his voice in her ear. She could air her thoughts and get the truth about Vanu off her chest. Yes, she'd have to live with the consequences of that decision, but could that be any worse that sitting in this prickly nest of lies and half truths?

She sat up and eased her feet down onto the cool tile floor. Pressed her hand to her belly for a moment for strength, even though she wasn't sure whether her sudden plan would be good or bad for her baby.

She crept across the dark room and found her phone where it lay on top of the dresser. She rarely used it, since she usually went to see her friends and her mom in person for a chat, like most people in Rahiri.

But L.A. was too far away for a drop-in visit.

She picked up the phone with a steady hand. It was after 2:00 a.m., so past midnight in L.A. Not a great time for a call.

Her heart pumped faster. She should really put the phone down and go back to bed.

Instead she opened the top drawer and pulled out a folded piece of paper. She didn't have AJ's address and phone number in L.A.—why would she?—but she'd found them in the old leather-bound address book Priia kept on her study desk. She wasn't sure at the time why she wanted them, just that she did. She'd already mapped AJ's address on the computer and peeped at the "bird's-eye view" of his sleek apartment building, like a spy on a covert mission.

She murmured his phone number like a mantra, knowing that at any time she could invoke him—live and in person—with a few pressed buttons. She knew from watching him that AJ answered nearly every call he got, which was a lot, so she was fairly sure he'd pick up at any time of the day or night.

And after midnight he'd be home alone.

At least she hoped he would. Fear flashed through her. What if he'd forgotten her already and was lost in the arms of a lascivious starlet?

She inhaled a deep breath and pressed the cool phone to her mouth for a moment. Didn't matter. She wasn't calling to beg him to come back, or tell him she loved him and couldn't live without him. Her only goal was to tell him the truth about Vanu, just because it felt right.

And to hear his voice one last time.

Her trembling fingertips had trouble hitting the right buttons on the tiny phone and she misdialed twice before she finally got the number right.

It rang. Why had she decided to call so late at night? It was rude. He'd probably be annoyed. Her thumb hovered over the disconnect button while her breath caught in her lungs.

Then he answered. "Hello." The sound of his voice sent a shock wave of emotion through her. She didn't know what to say.

"Hello, AJ."

"Lani." He sounded shocked. He could probably tell from the number that the call was from Rahiri, but he obviously didn't know it was her. They'd never talked on the phone before.

"Yes, it's me." Her head swam with such a tangle of thoughts that her mind went completely blank. "How are you?"

"Getting along. Keeping busy. How are you?"

Lani paced her bedroom. This wasn't how it was supposed to go. Phony pleasantries exchanged like strangers. "I'm fine." She wanted to say so much more, to shout it. To pour out her feelings and tell him how much she missed him.

"And the baby?"

"Good. At least I think so. I have a doctor's appointment tomorrow, but I've been feeling pretty good." Except for the nausea, but that probably was stress this time. "I'm sorry to call so late."

"Is Mom okay?" His voice filled with concern. He must be wondering exactly why she would call in the middle of the night.

"Yes. She's really busy with the coronation plans. She misses you, of course." She then regretted saying that, like she was trying to prod him to guilt. She really should get to the point before she lost her nerve and kept the truth to herself forever. "I called to tell you something."

"Oh?" He sounded reserved. What did he think she would say? That she loved him and wanted him to come back? Her face heated. If only her thoughts would stop running away with her.

"It's that…" she hesitated. How did you tell someone that you hated their brother? "Vanu and me… We didn't…we weren't…" Words hovered just out of reach. AJ was totally silent at the other end. "I didn't love him."

AJ said nothing. She could imagine him frowning. Thinking.

"I didn't like him." Emboldened by his silence, she went on. "He was cold to me, cruel, even." She swallowed, and walked back across the dark bedroom. "I hated him."

The harsh words fell from her lips easily, then hung in the air like a judgment. Cold dread trickled through her. She couldn't take the truth back now.

"What did you say?" AJ's voice was low, almost a whisper.

Lani froze. Was he horrified by her blunt confession? Disgusted by her lack of compassion for his dead brother? "I'm sorry. Maybe I shouldn't have said it. I know he's your brother and even if he wasn't I shouldn't speak ill of the dead. Now you know what I'm really like. See? I'm not nice at all like you thought and I have evil thoughts inside my head and—"

"I hated him, too." AJ's words rang bold and clear through the phone.

"What?" She spun around, startled.

"I hated him. *Hated* him. What did he do to you?" Sudden concern tightened his voice. "Did he hurt you?"

"Not physically, at least not that much. But he was cruel. He'd taunt me and belittle me, then be all smiles if there was anyone around."

"I don't believe it." AJ sounded incredulous.

Her shoulders stiffened. "It's true."

He laughed. "I don't mean that I don't believe *you*. I believe you completely, because that's exactly what he used to do to me."

"You never said anything."

"Nor did you."

"I didn't want to offend you."

"Same here." He let out a loud guffaw. "I can't believe we were dancing carefully around Vanu's memory when neither of us could stand him."

"Your mom has no idea he was like that." Lani drew in a deep breath. "I didn't want her to find out, either."

"I used to tell her, back when I was a kid, and she never believed me, anyway. He was always her sweet little princeling. He really knew how to turn it on when he wanted to."

"I know. It was like living with two completely different people. The public Vanu and the private one." Relief rolled through Lani, warm and soothing. "I tried to make him happy, but after a while I realized it was hurting me that made him happy." She stiffened when she remembered their last encounter, the one that had left her pregnant. Why shouldn't AJ know about that, too? She didn't want him to think she'd lain willingly in Vanu's arms after all he'd done to her over the years.

"I didn't want to conceive a child with him." She hesitated for a moment, wondering how he'd take what she was about to say. "He forced himself on me, said he was my husband and could do whatever he wanted. That it was his right."

She knew it wasn't about love, or even pleasure, for Vanu. It was about inflicting pain, abusing his power.

"He raped you." AJ's voice was hoarse. "If he was still alive I'd kill him. He was a sociopath. I didn't realize that until long after I'd gone, of course, and had time to get some distance. He's given me great inspiration for my movie villains over the years. I always thought it was lucky he didn't have any real interest in ruling the country, or he might have turned into a dictator."

"I think he was too lazy for that." Lani laughed, a weird, high-pitched sound, more a release of tension than anything else. "And he really didn't like people. I suspect he found it a lot of work pretending to be normal."

"So why did you cry when you learned he was dead?"

"Relief. I was dreading the awful possibility that he'd come back and make me miserable again. All those mornings of waking up to his angry face and hearing him criticize everything I did."

AJ let out a long sigh. "How come you didn't tell anyone Vanu was a sadistic bastard? Were you going to stay married to him forever if he hadn't died?"

Lani blew out. "I was trying to be brave. I didn't want to hurt your mom and let down the royal family by causing a scandal. My mom always made a big deal about how a woman should never air her dirty laundry. She never spoke about her own marriage and divorce." She shoved a hand through her hair. "I knew I was taking on a big responsibility when I married the future king. I guess I figured I'd have to live with my mistake."

There was a silence. "Just like you would have lived with your duty to marry me, if I hadn't left."

Lani didn't know what to say. It was true. As she'd gotten to know AJ, she'd realized the duty would have been a pleasure. She didn't want to push her luck by saying that, though. She'd called to tell him how she felt about Vanu, not to put pressure on him to do anything about it.

"Why did you decide to tell me now?" AJ's voice had an odd sound to it.

Lani swallowed. "I don't know exactly. I just wanted to tell you the truth."

"The truth. That's been an elusive little… Don't go anywhere."

"What do you mean?"

"Don't leave the palace."

"Why not?" She glanced over her shoulder. She felt under siege all the time lately, with press everywhere and people taking photos of her whenever she even looked out the window.

"So I know where to find you." His voice had a ring of command to it.

Why did he want to find her? Did he plan to come and scold her for keeping the truth hidden all this time? She'd only been trying to protect the family name.

The truth had been her enemy since she'd come to this palace. She'd danced around it, skirted it and fluffed over it so many times since she'd had the misfortune to marry Vanu. And there was one powerful truth she still kept locked tight in her heart.

She'd never told AJ that she loved him.

"Joe, you still got that jet out at Burbank?" AJ marched across the room, picking up items of clothing and tossing them into his bag.

"Do you know what time it is?" His friend's gruff voice assaulted him down the phone. He and Joe had shared a house when AJ was in film school—two kids with too much money and no sense of direction. They'd seen each other through more than a few scrapes since. Joe was now a successful film agent with a passion for cars and planes.

"Late, yeah. I can wait until dawn to leave, though." Every moment away from Lani was agonizing right now, but no need to torment other people with his desperation.

"Dawn? What the heck are you talking about? Where do you need to go in such a rush?"

"Home. Rahiri."

"I thought you'd decided once and for all that L.A. was your home." Joe's voice softened a bit.

"It's complicated. Anyway, I need to get to Rahiri as soon as humanly possible."

He heard a long sigh. "Let me guess, that gorgeous almost-wife of yours is involved somehow."

"Lani. Yes, I need to see her." And touch her, and hold her and kiss her—if she'd let him.

Joe chuckled. "I think everyone in America wants to see her, given the amount of media coverage she's getting. I doubt most of them had even heard of Rahiri until the two of you became such media darlings."

"Why am I friends with you?"

"Because I have a plane, apparently. And yes, I'll take you, but not until first light."

"I love you, Joe."

"And I'm not the only one you love, from the sound of things. See you on the tarmac." Joe hung up the phone.

AJ drew in a deep steadying breath. In only a few hours he'd see Lani again. Hearing her voice had undone all his hard work of trying to move on. Not that he'd been at all successful. He couldn't even stand to talk to her anymore. The distance between them was too agonizing and he had to see her right away. He didn't want to exchange one more word with her until they were face-to-face. Too easy for misunderstandings and complications to arise.

It was still dark when he arrived at the airport, but he wasn't surprised to see the lights on inside his friend's beloved plane. Joe was outside checking out some piece of machinery and he laughed when he saw AJ. "I knew you'd be here at least an hour early."

AJ shrugged.

"Lucky thing I came out here right when I hung up the phone—and she's ready to go."

"I really do love you." AJ grinned and heaved his bag inside the tiny cockpit.

By the time dawn came they were already out over the ocean, and the tentative rays of sun illuminated the featureless plain of dark water. They stopped to refuel and grab a late breakfast in Hawaii. Another seven hours or so of empty ocean and they'd be there.

His heart rate increased as they passed the first of the green, sand-fringed islands that dotted the route to Rahiri like giant stepping stones.

Would Lani resent him for ruining all their careful plans and leaving her in the lurch?

Of course she would. She'd borne the brunt of all the insatiable media curiosity that stood his hair on end—while dealing with pregnancy and the organizational and emotional drama of preparing to become Rahiri's official monarch.

But she'd called him. At a time when no one else would know and—as far as he could tell—with no hidden agenda other than to air the ugly truth she'd kept hidden all along.

She hadn't asked him to come back, but right now nothing could stop him.

"Is this a round-trip excursion or are you staying

for good this time?" Joe's voice jolted him from his thoughts.

"It all depends."

"On Lani the lovely."

"You got it." He wouldn't force himself on her. He'd always resolved not to do that. Rahiian or not, every woman deserved to choose her own husband.

"Speaking from personal experience, I've learned that women will let you make a mistake once, but they don't look too kindly on you screwing up the same way a second time. What made you change your mind about her?"

AJ hesitated. He'd probably mentioned his older brother to Joe in passing a few times, but had never revealed the full extent of his malice. In general he preferred to leave Vanu buried in the past. But was that perpetuating the fraud that had driven him and Lani apart? Still, he didn't want to say anything without asking Lani. If she wanted the ugly details of her first marriage kept secret, he'd oblige.

"Maybe I just came to my senses."

"Don't lose 'em again, okay? This is a long flight to make at a moment's notice." Joe turned and shoved him.

"I'm living and learning every day, bro. This time I plan to get it right."

"I did warn you that marriage isn't for the faint of heart?" Joe had been married three times and, by his account, paid untold amounts of alimony to his three former beloveds.

"Many a time. You're probably at least fifty percent responsible for scaring me off marriage until now. That and the fact that the divorce rate in L.A. is around seventy percent."

"What's the divorce rate like in Rahiri?"

"I have no idea. Haven't lived there in a decade. Lani's mom was divorced, though I suppose that took place in the States."

"You just make sure it doesn't happen to you."

"I'd have to be married first." A possibility that had blossomed in his mind again. Sure, it would be easier if it weren't for the whole royalty angle, but the prospect of making Lani his wife made his chest swell with excitement.

The sun was climbing across the sky by the time Rahiri came into view, its familiar teardrop-shaped outline beckoning him like an old friend. "Skip the airport and head straight for the palace. There's a long paved drive with palm trees on each side. You can land right there."

"And get a royal summons? I'd rather go to the airport."

"Too far away. It's almost an hour's drive from the palace."

"I thought that was so their royal majesties don't have to be troubled by the drone of engines."

"It is, but I'm sure they'll survive."

"Your mom was really pissed off last time." They'd done it once before, years ago, when AJ returned for a family party with a group of friends.

"I can handle her. I already called and told her we were coming in. Didn't want to get shot at on approach now that everyone's so paranoid these days. She wasn't happy about it, but she'll survive." AJ scanned the ground through the small side window. Already he could make out the multilayered rooftops of the palace and the lush grounds. Lani was down there somewhere. How would she react when she saw him?

Joe guided the plane expertly into a straight line with the drive, which was mercifully free of vehicles and pedestrians. "Here goes nothing."

As they roared to the ground and taxied down the drive, AJ's pulse went into overdrive. As soon as the plane stopped, people came running out of the palace. He jumped from the plane, scanning the faces.

"AJ!" His mother's scream rose above the din of voices. "Didn't I tell you never to land on the drive? It's dangerous—there could be a pothole, or a fallen tree branch."

"Palm trees don't have branches, Mom." He gave her a hug. "Where's Lani?"

"She's being measured for her coronation gown. They're doing it in the ballroom because of the good light in there. Hey, where are you going?"

AJ had already slipped her grasp and strode into the palace, heading for the ballroom. Staff members stared at him, and hushed whispers buzzed amongst the polite greetings.

He had no idea how Lani would respond to his sudden arrival, but at this point he really didn't care, he just ached to see her. The palace corridors seemed endless as he marched along them, past the secret passageway he'd sneaked into with Lani, past all the other doorways and hallways where they'd exchanged glances—and more.

"Did you return to claim the throne?" A black-clad reporter, brandishing a tiny video camera, leaped out of a doorway to his left.

"How did you get in?" AJ lunged toward him, responding instinctively to the invasion of privacy.

"Couldn't stand to see your brother's wife claim

the throne?" A female reporter darted up behind him, holding up a camera phone.

AJ grappled with the first man, getting him in an armlock. "Guards! There's an intruder."

People rushed around them, servants hurried along the corridors and reporters poured in through the unsecured and glassless windows that ringed the palace and linked it to the gardens outside.

AJ grappled with a smelly man in a plaid shirt and yelled to the servants to make sure none of the scum got anywhere near Lani. Reporters who'd been hanging around the palace bored out of their skulls for weeks surged in after the others, shutters whirring and microphones thrust in his face.

"Are you back for good?"

"Is *Dragon Chaser Five* going to start shooting?"

"Did you fly the plane yourself?"

"Is the baby really yours?"

"Did you miss Lani?"

This last question made him look up, and his eyes met the beady blue ones of a blond reporter he vaguely recognized.

"I did miss Lani."

The scrum of reporters suddenly hushed.

"Did you come back for her?"

"I came back to see her." He didn't want to claim more than that. He wasn't sure if Lani even would see him, after he'd promised to marry her—in front of the whole world—then welshed on the deal.

"Do you want to marry her?"

"I think that's a bit premature. I…" Something caught his eye behind the reporter's head and he looked into the long hall leading to the interior of the palace.

Lani. Flanked by two guards, standing only a few feet away. Her face was blank, expressionless.

Blood rushed to AJ's muscles and he pushed through the crush of reporters. He'd imagined her so many times, soft honey eyes, long silky hair hiding her slim figure, her hesitant walk and sweet laugh and his vision seemed conjured to life in front of him.

But as he approached her, Lani seemed to shrink from him. She glanced at the reporters behind him— why were they still there? Couldn't the guards throw them out?

"Let's go somewhere we can talk."

She nodded.

He turned to the guards. "Make sure they don't follow us." He reached out to take Lani's arm, then noticed how stiffly she held her body and pulled it back. What did she think of his sudden appearance?

Nine

Lani marched as fast as she could beside AJ. Her thoughts ran in all directions. Why was he here, and so suddenly? Hope mingled with terror and anticipation as they drew farther away from the crowd of crazy reporters and into the quiet recesses of the palace.

"In here." AJ opened a door into the darkened throne room. She stepped past him, agonizingly conscious of his big, broad physique and the energy that always crackled in the air between them.

None of the hundred sconces or the incongruously high-tech video conferencing equipment was turned on, and the only light came through a small skylight in the ceiling. The massive "throne"—a squarish chunk of black basalt etched with symbols so ancient that no one could actually read them—hulked in the middle of the room.

AJ closed the door quietly behind them. The shaft

of light from overhead threw his strong features into high relief, including the frown etched in his brow. "I had to come right away, to apologize."

"For what?" He had much to apologize for, but she didn't want to jump to any conclusions.

That, and she didn't know what else to say.

"I feel like such an ass. Why couldn't I see it?" AJ turned and paced across the room, disappearing into the semi-darkness. "Why didn't I realize that Vanu had made your life hell, too?"

"I kept it secret." Her voice was almost a whisper in the vast chamber. "Until I couldn't keep it secret any longer."

"Before your middle-of-the-night phone call, I didn't even realize what I'd done." He strode back across the darkened room. "That I'd let my own fears and insecurities get the better of me. I didn't want to live a life being second-best, the backup, the understudy after the tragic loss of my glorious brother who was loved and missed by all."

His eyes gleamed in the half light, and he let out a snort of disbelief. "But that brother never existed at all—except in my own mind, as my tormentor. The man who died was a small and petty individual who lived for his own amusement. That man can't keep me from Rahiri—or from you."

He drew her into his arms, and she rested her head against his broad chest, feeling protected and comforted for the first time since Vanu's boat was found. Desire flared inside her like a spark under an encouraging breath.

"I missed your smile." AJ brushed his thumb over her mouth—her smile appeared magically beneath his touch.

Lani leaned into him. "I missed your laugh." The palace had seemed so empty, so dull and lifeless despite all the staff bustling to and fro.

"I missed laughing. I haven't done much lately." He stroked her back, and his fingers stirred up rivers of sensation. She'd tried so hard to forget the feelings he aroused in her, and she couldn't keep them from flooding back.

"Me, either."

His lips hovered just over hers, close enough so she could feel their heat. Excitement buzzed in the air and made her skin tingle. Was it real? Could AJ really be back? Was everything going to be okay?

It seemed too much to hope for. Still, he was here, with his arms wrapped around her. Something she'd dreamed of in spite of herself the whole time he was gone.

"I missed your kisses," she whispered.

"I missed yours." He swiped a kiss close to her lips, but not quite on them. Her lips stung at the sudden and unexpected denial. "But maybe I don't deserve to have any more."

"You may not, but I do." She narrowed her eyes at him.

"So true." He lowered his lips gently over hers, slid his tongue provocatively between her lips and gave her a kiss that made her toes curl.

Her nipples tightened against his chest and she ran her hands over the ridged muscle of his back, enjoying his strength. It made her feel safe, though it shouldn't really, he hadn't made her any promises.

She'd learned not to count on anything for sure except the sweetness of the present moment. "I'm glad you came back," she whispered. Even if he didn't stay, she'd always have this moment to remember, when she felt safe and whole and loved, for a while.

AJ nuzzled her ear. "I missed you like crazy. I tried to put you out of my mind and to distract myself with the films and parties and all those things I used to enjoy, but I found I didn't want any of it any more. Not without you."

Her heart contracted painfully. "I missed you, too." She'd ached for him, night and day. "But you'd left me, and there was nothing I could do about it."

"Except phone me." He stroked her cheek.

"I was scared to tell the truth. I wasn't sure if you'd be angry, or think I was nuts."

"I am, and I do. I don't think you should have put up with any of that nonsense from Vanu." He lifted her chin until their eyes met. His gaze was filled with concern. "You should have told him he was a jerk and dumped him."

Lani swallowed. Left in her heart was the one truth she'd never told anyone. "I did."

"What?"

She pushed back, separating herself from AJ inch by inch. "I told him, that night, after he…forced himself on me…that he could kill me if he wanted but that I wouldn't stay married to him for another day. I told him I hated him." The memory of her own voice, shrill and serious in the night, made her shiver.

AJ stared at her. "And that's why he left. Why he went out on the boat."

"And why he died." Her words, spoken softly, rang like a tolling bell off the stone walls. "How did he die? No one's ever told me. Trying to spare my feelings or something."

He rubbed a hand over his mouth and looked away.

"Anyone's guess, really. There wasn't much left. Just the skeleton. A lot of animals and birds on that island."

She let the ghastly image sink in.

"It was definitely him, though. They checked the teeth against his dental records. He won't be back again."

She didn't know what to say or do. How could she be pleased to hear such grim news?

AJ reached for her hand. "It's not your fault he's dead."

She clenched her fist inside his grasp. "I wanted him dead." The words flew from her mouth. "It's ugly but it's the truth and I can't change that."

"It's his fault that you felt like that, and I could kill him again myself for putting that sadness and guilt into your heart. You need to let go of it."

"I want to. Maybe that's why I had to tell you the truth. I had to tell someone."

"Were you worried I wouldn't believe you?"

"A little." She hesitated and watched his expression. "And I was a little afraid that you wouldn't care."

"Because I ran out on you?"

She nodded.

"But now you know that I did that because of my own past with Vanu. I gave up telling people about it a long time ago. I wanted to leave him in my past." He reached toward her and stroked her shoulder. "I think we should both do that."

Lani swallowed. "We can't."

"Why not?"

"Because I'm still carrying his baby."

AJ's eyes dropped to her belly, which was still barely more than flat. "It's hard to believe there's a whole person in there, getting ready for life."

Lani swallowed. Did he now intend to be a father to that tiny person, or simply an uncle? She didn't dare ask.

He frowned, thoughtful. "Your baby won't be raised by Vanu. All of his or her genes come from my mother and father, just like mine, and from you. There's no reason why Vanu should cast a shadow over the child's life. We'll raise it with affection and love."

"And if he or she does have any problems or issues, we won't pretend they don't exist. We'll do our best to help. I've had enough of trying to pretend things are perfect when they aren't. I've spent way too much time trying to be nice and make everything go smoothly, and all my efforts nearly ruined everything. Trying to make everything perfect by glossing over the truth is at the root of all of our problems."

"You're right." He tilted his head. "And I've spent my adult life creating and maintaining elaborate fantasies for the screen. I guess my childhood prepared me really well for that."

Lani filled her lungs with air. "From now on we'll face problems head-on, and talk to each other honestly about them."

"That's a promise." AJ stared at her, his expression unreadable. "I love you, Lani."

She froze. The words entered her brain, but it didn't know what to make of them. What did love even mean? She'd tried to love Vanu, and failed miserably. She had strong feelings for AJ, but she'd told herself time and time again since he left that they were most definitely not love.

It wasn't until he'd gone and left her alone again that she'd realized she loved him.

He reached for her hand and she let him take it. He must have noticed it was trembling slightly.

She didn't know what to say. She wanted to say, "I love you, too," but it seemed too much, too soon, when she didn't even know what his intentions were.

And despite all her exhortations to get real, she was afraid to ask.

Words failing her, she stepped forward and kissed him hard on the mouth. Too much emotion. She couldn't process all the strange feelings roiling in her mind and body.

AJ's arms around her waist sent heat flooding to her core. She clutched him closer, winding her fingers into the fabric of his shirt, then plucking and tugging at it until she pulled it loose from his pants.

Their kisses grew more frantic as she struggled with his buttons and clawed the fabric away from his chest. She yanked at his belt buckle, hating that she had to pull back even a few inches to get her hands on it. She just wanted to bury herself in AJ's large body, to lose herself in him and revel in the sheer fact that he was right here, right now.

Her nipples stung and tingled with intense arousal as they brushed against his bare chest through the thin fabric of her dress. AJ's hands roamed over her as she kissed his face and his neck and pushed his shirt off over his muscled arms and back.

His eyes gleamed with passion as he undid the fastening on her dress and let it fall to the floor.

Impatient with his stiff jeans, Lani pushed and shoved at them until they fell past his powerful thighs and he stepped out of them and stood, clothed only in the pale light drifting through the skylight above.

Lani shivered in anticipation at the sight of his

arousal. AJ pulled her to him, his chest heaving. He lowered his mouth over hers and took her in a kiss that sucked the breath from her lungs. Lani kissed him back with all the emotion she'd locked away deep inside her after he left. All the pain and hurt mingled with affection and passion and exploded over them both, locking them together in a powerful embrace that shut out the world.

Lani felt AJ lifting her off the floor, carrying her in his strong arms. She didn't open her eyes, just let him take her wherever he wanted. It felt good to stop planning and worrying and scheming and simply go with him.

He set her down in a sitting position on a smooth, stone surface that contrasted intriguingly with the hot, yielding strength of his body. The sensation made her wriggle against him, as he stood in front of her, his erection level with her very aroused sex.

"Now," she pleaded, gripping him gently with her fingers. She needed to feel him inside her. She wanted him to fill the gap he'd left when he went away.

AJ entered her slowly, pulling her to the edge of the stone and wrapping her legs around his waist. She groaned as he sank deep inside her and a sensation of relief and joy filled her from the inside out. She pressed her body against his and hugged him tight as he moved slowly inside her.

I love him.

The words filled her brain as the notion filled her heart. Again. Was that enough? It should be. Love— and whatever those other sensations were called—filled her to overflowing and made her gasp as AJ moved over her.

He kissed her gently, then firmer, and lifted her up

so she was in his arms, still moving with him. She felt light as a feather, supported by his powerful frame. Her arms and legs still wrapped around him, AJ eased himself into position on the stone surface so she was sitting on top of him, her feet resting on the throne.

AJ sucked her neck and she arched her back, taking him deeper still. She found she was able to move over him easily, keeping a tight hold around his neck and back, and moving up and down with her feet. Moving faster, and then slower, she let emotions and sensations cascade over her.

Pure pleasure trickled through her body and she wanted to enjoy it to the fullest. She'd known so little pleasure in the last few years that it was like a precious jewel she wanted to hold and admire for as long as she could.

Judging from the sounds he was making—earthy groans and whispered endearments—AJ was enjoying it, too. His hands moved tirelessly over her skin, stroking and supporting at the same time.

She kissed him, thrusting her tongue into his mouth in time with her movements. The sensation was cheeky and delicious. With AJ she could take risks and do silly, fun things without worrying about being judged or scolded.

She peppered kisses all over his face and ran her hands through his thick, silky hair, drinking in the masculine scent of his warm, sweaty skin. She loved the rough feel of his cheek against hers, the firm pressure of his fingers on her skin.

Although her climax hovered so close she could almost feel the convulsions, she delayed it. She slowed the pace, pulled back just as she was about to burst. Part of her wanted to forge ahead and taste the sweetness of their joint explosion, but the rest of her wanted to prolong this blissful experience as long as she could.

She still didn't know why AJ had come back, or for how long. He'd said he loved her, but she knew love wasn't always enough. Right now that didn't matter. What she shared with AJ was already so much more wonderful than anything she'd experienced in her years of marriage, and if it was all she got, she could live with that.

She kissed him, drinking in his scent and tasting the sweetness of his kiss as if this was the last time she'd touch him. Savored each precious millisecond of his hands on her skin and his hard belly pressed to her soft one. She moved so slowly, as if she could alter the passage of time and prolong the present moment infinitely.

"You're torturing me." AJ's whispered words tickled her ear.

"Maybe you deserve it." She trailed a light fingernail along his spine.

"I do." He nipped at her ear. "But you could encourage me to be a bad boy more often with this kind of punishment."

Lani pressed her breasts into his chest, enjoying the sting of pleasure in her nipples. "Maybe I will. It seems I enjoy inflicting torment." She shifted her weight slightly, and felt him move inside her.

"I should have known there was more to you than meets the eye."

She opened her eyes and met his dark gaze. "I warned you when we first met."

"You did." He narrowed his eyes and raked them down her body, causing her skin to tingle. "Maybe that's what intrigued me. Then the way you kissed me…"

"You could tell I had a dark side."

"Or a delicious side. Either one worked for me." AJ licked her mouth and she shuddered in response.

She pressed her mouth to his ear. "Do you think it's possible we bring out the worst in each other?"

"Absolutely." He lifted her chin with his thumb so he was looking into her eyes again. "Why else would we be making love on our nation's ancient throne?"

Lani gasped and looked down. "Oh, no."

"Oh, yes. What did you think we were sitting on?"

"I don't know." She frowned. "I didn't think."

AJ's mischievous chuckle rocked them both. "I never would have imagined it could be so...comfortable. I can't help wondering if anyone's done this before."

Lani let a wry smile lift her mouth. "We really don't know that much about the customs and culture of the Old Ones. Maybe this is exactly what they did on it."

"Very wise of them, in my opinion. Perhaps we could revive the custom."

"Apparently we already have."

AJ shifted his weight and moved deeper inside her. Lani arched her back and shuddered, again dancing just microseconds from release. Could this really be a new beginning? If AJ stayed and became king, almost anything was possible, for Rahiri as well as for her.

Are you staying?

The words hovered just behind her lips, but she swallowed them back, afraid to spoil everything. He'd come back, and that was enough.

She leaned into him and started to move again, letting the delicious sensations pulse through her until she started to lose control. This time she didn't stop, but pushed them both over the edge of pleasure into the strange, dark, powerful, empty space beyond, where thoughts and feelings collapsed and their bodies became one.

When she finally opened her eyes again, they were both lying back on the polished basalt. She'd never realized how big the great stone was. Side by side, holding hands, they lay under the skylight, the surface oddly soft beneath their totally relaxed limbs.

Lani turned to look at AJ. "What if we've just broken an ancient taboo?"

AJ's mouth swept into a naughty grin. "I'd say ancient taboos are pretty much made to be broken."

A volley of sharp knocks on the carved wooden door jerked her into a sitting position. "Someone's coming."

AJ didn't move. "Not surprising. We did kind of disappear on them."

She jumped off the stone and scrambled back into her dress. "Come on! We don't want them to know what we were doing."

"Why not? It's not a crime."

"It might be if the throne is involved."

"If I become king I can grant us absolution." He eased his pants over his powerful thighs. "Same if you become queen. Though we'd have to decide if we deserve the pardon."

Lani ran fingers through her tangled hair. Now he was just messing with her mind. Unless he didn't entirely know what was on his own mind—which was more than likely. Everything had happened so fast. It was less than twenty-four hours ago that she'd phoned him with her revelation.

More banging on the door made her jump.

"Don't worry, it's locked." AJ winked at her.

She pulled her sandals on. "What shall we say we were doing in here?"

"Hmm." AJ buttoned up his shirt very slowly. "Maybe we could tell them that we couldn't decide who should take the throne, so we both decided to try it out and see how it felt."

"You're terrible!"

"Trust me, I know that. It's the truth, though, isn't it?"

"We haven't discussed who should take the throne." She peered at him.

"Do you want to be queen?" He stopped buttoning and stared at her.

Only if you're king. "Not really. I've been rather railroaded into it."

"Well, that's how it happens, isn't it?" He smiled and went back to buttoning. "In some societies people are stabbing each other in the back trying to seize the throne. In others, we're all keen to dodge the crown that's being thrust upon us." He tucked in his shirt, then stared straight ahead. "I admit I've felt bad about that, too."

"You regretted giving up the crown."

"The crown I could care less about. It's Rahiri I regretted losing. This is a great little nation and it could be even better. Sure, the elders have the people's best interests in their hearts, but they don't have the energy and vision of a younger person who's lived in another culture and been exposed to new ideas."

"I'd been thinking about that. We need more female doctors, and why can't the elders be women, too?"

"You are prepared to take on the role of queen." AJ looked at her, a hint of surprise in his eyes.

Had she said the wrong thing? Would he think she

didn't want him there because she'd been ready to rule the nation? She shrugged. "I had to prepare. I didn't really have a choice."

He frowned. "You're the one person who's never really had a choice in any of this. What do you want, Lani?"

You.

Why couldn't she say it? It was just one word, but it ducked and hid behind her tongue. What was she so afraid of? That she'd scare him away?

"You don't like giving away anything about yourself." He cocked his head and surveyed her through narrowed eyes. "You figure your secrets are safer if you keep them locked away inside."

"I told you the truth about my marriage to Vanu."

"That was a good start, but I want to know about you. What you think, and what you really want."

Another thunderous knock on the door was accompanied by a shout. "Is anyone in there? We're going to break the door down."

"Oh, no." Lani scuttled behind the stone.

"Don't break it down." AJ's voice boomed off the high walls. "I'm in here with Lani and we're both fine."

Are we? The warm glow of lust had dimmed, leaving Lani anxious and apprehensive. All this talking seemed to be tying them up in knots. She'd never been good with words. She certainly couldn't talk easily about herself.

"You didn't answer my question, Lani." AJ ignored the commotion outside, looking only at her. "What do you want?"

What if she told him she wanted him to stay, and he did but was unhappy? Would it be her fault?

"Stop hiding your thoughts from me." AJ stepped toward her. "You're just complicating everything further."

"I want you to stay and become king." She pushed the words out with great effort. Relief mingled with terror formed a fog in her brain.

AJ's expression didn't soften. "That's about me. What about *you?*"

I want to be your wife.

No. There was absolutely no way on this ocean-covered earth she could say that. It would amount to asking him to marry her. She'd never do that.

"Why can't you say it?" AJ put his hand on her shoulder. His dark gaze seemed to pierce her skin, making her even more uncomfortable.

"Because I don't know what I want. I only know I don't want you to go." The words burst from her on a sob. "Maybe I really am too shallow, or too silly for you. You expect me to have all these grand thoughts about my destiny and lots of big dreams or something." She shoved a tear aside. "But I don't. Maybe I am just a simple village girl. I only want to raise my baby and be happy."

AJ stared at her. Tears ran down her cheeks and she didn't try to stop them. That really was the truth about her and if he hoped for more he was doomed to disappointment.

Maybe that's what she'd been trying to hide all along. "I'm not educated or even particularly intelligent." Lord knows Vanu had made a point of that often enough. "I just do my best to help the people around me and try to do the right thing. And sometimes the right thing doesn't feel right at all…" A violent sob racked her body.

"Don't put yourself down, Lani. You're brave and strong—look at all you've endured—and I firmly believe you're capable of anything. Whatever you do, don't let Vanu's opinion of you shape your view of yourself. I'd be nowhere if I'd done that."

"And you're an award-winning director." Another tear dripped off her chin. "That's a big accomplishment." No wonder he didn't want to abandon the career he'd worked so hard to build.

"Being a director is a lot like being a king, really." He thumbed a tear off her cheek. "You have to keep a lot of different people happy while guiding them all in the direction of your vision. I'm beginning to realize that my film career has been the perfect preparation for the job I'm truly intended to do."

"Wouldn't you miss Hollywood and all the excitement of the industry?"

"Not the way I missed you and Rahiri while I was back there." His soft voice tugged at something deep inside her. There was something different in his eyes now, too. A reflective look she didn't remember seeing before.

"I truly think I was meant to live there for a while, and I did enjoy myself—almost as much as the media claimed—but now it's my time to come home."

The last word hung in the air and reverberated off the stone floor.

Then the powerful moment was interrupted by more fevered banging on the door. "AJ Rahia, come here right now!"

"Your mom." Lani couldn't help laughing. "She's probably run out of spin for the reporters."

"Is that any way to talk to the king?" AJ raised a brow. Humor twinkled in his eyes.

Lani drew in a breath. "Are you really going to stay and become king?"

"Only if you'll be my queen." He took her hands in his and held her gaze while he dropped to one knee. "Lani, will you marry me?"

Ten

AJ held his breath while two more fat crystal tears slid down Lani's cheeks.

"I missed you so much, A.J. I almost couldn't stand it when you left. I wanted to be mad at you for abandoning me, but I couldn't. You're the most caring and tender man I've ever met and…" She drew in a shaky breath. "I love you."

His heart squeezed. She hadn't answered his question, though. Did she still worry that he felt forced into marrying her?

"I love you, too, Lani. And I want to marry you because I'd like to be your husband, not because a nation expects it of me. Your beauty seduced me from the first moment I met you, but your generous and giving spirit stole my heart. I want to spend the rest of my life with you."

AJ reached into his pocket and pulled out a wad of

tissue paper. It wasn't easy unwrapping it while keeping a tight hold on her with one hand. He was still half-afraid she'd run off, or just evaporate into the humid air. His good fortune at winning her back seemed too sweet to be real.

At last he managed to free the sparkly gem he'd had to twist arms to obtain in the middle of the night.

Lani gasped when she saw it. "Oh, my goodness, that's beautiful."

"It had better be. It's from L.A.'s finest jeweler."

"You had this planned?"

He hesitated. Did he want her to think he'd been planning this proposal since the day he left and spent days agonizing over ring designs?

No. The truth was what brought them together and what would hold them together into the future.

"Only since 2:00 a.m. I had to drag my friend Niall out of bed. He's a jewelry designer and I knew he'd have something fabulous enough to be fit for a queen." The enormous cushion-cut rock had made even AJ's jaded eyes pop. "Shall we see if it fits?"

Lani nodded, eyes wide. He held her hand gently and pushed the delicate gold band onto her ring finger. The ring slid on easily, then the heavy gem tilted to one side. "It's a bit big."

"We'll get it fixed. It's beautiful and I love it." Her eyes glistened with tears again. "And yes, I will marry you."

AJ picked her up and twirled her around. He must have had the biggest grin in the world on his face.

"AJ, sweetheart—" The voice was not Lani's but his mom's, coming from the other side of the door.

"Do you think she's been listening at the door?" he whispered.

Lani smiled. "Probably. I forgot she was there."

"Me, too. I forget about everything when you're around." He gave her a squeeze. "You think we should let her in on the good news?"

Lani tensed a little in his arms.

"Or are you not quite ready to face the mayhem again?"

She shrugged. "We'll have to sooner or later. Might as well get it over with." She rubbed at her cheeks, and he smoothed away any last telltale signs of her tears. He took her hand and they marched toward the door, which locked from the inside with a massive iron bolt. He pulled the bolt, then caught Lani's hand again as he opened the door and light flooded into the dim chamber.

As expected, a large crowd had gathered outside, flanking his mom, who had those bright spots of color high on her cheeks that let him know she was really agitated.

"Hi, Mom."

"What were you doing in there?" His mom glanced at Lani, who blushed.

"That's between me and Lani and the throne." He cocked his head and gave Lani a sly wink.

Her flush deepened.

He felt strangely calm. "I've come back for good, and Lani has kindly agreed to marry me."

His mom's mouth fell open and she gasped. Then she grasped Lani in her arms and hugged her. "What wonderful news!"

Photographic flashes half blinded him.

"Who's going to rule Rahiri?" A British accent.

AJ held Lani close. "Both of us. We'll rule together until our child comes of age."

"But isn't the baby your brother Vanu's?" An American woman shoved a microphone under his nose.

"Vanu's gone." He glanced at Lani. "I'll raise the child as a father and love him or her as my own until they're old enough to rule."

"Will you keep making films?" a young man shouted from near the back.

"I will. I already have some ideas for films set in Rahiri."

He looked at Lani, whose eyes widened. Then she smiled. "It would be a shame for AJ to waste his creative talents. And there's a wealth of talent on this island that will enjoy working on the films."

AJ put his arm around her. "Rahiri's changed a lot since I was a boy. We have better schools and hospitals. We have cell phones and satellite TV. But the important things have stayed the same. People care about each other and about the land and water they live on. We have customs and culture totally unique to Rahiri that we celebrate and enjoy just as our ancestors did. Lani and I look forward to continuing the legacies of both progress and tradition that my father set in motion."

Cameras flashed and AJ smiled. Already he felt rather relaxed in the new role. Different aspects of their lives seemed to be slotting into place in a neat yet interesting pattern, much like the colorful woven fabrics of Lani's dresses, or the ornate teak carvings on the veranda around them.

They answered more questions together, Lani growing more confident and talkative, her beauty radiant as the noon sunshine.

Finally AJ decided it was time for some peace and quiet. "Now I must ask you to all leave the palace. The family needs some privacy."

* * *

Lani's nose tickled a bit as Priia dusted the traditional pollen on her cheeks with a fat makeup brush.

"It makes you glow so nicely! We should all wear it every day." Her mother-in-law beamed.

"I'm not sure the bees would appreciate that, but it does feel soft." Just like her silk dress, an intricate weave of delicate colors and real gold thread. She'd worn a similar dress for her wedding to Vanu, but this time everything felt different, maybe because it wasn't all strange and alarming like the first time. She knew everyone at the palace and it was already her home. The ceremony marked the happy change of welcoming AJ into her life.

The population of Rahiri swelled to almost double its usual numbers for the joint wedding and coronation. She rarely watched TV but now she made a special effort to avoid it. It was too bizarre to see herself cast in the "rags to riches to happiness" drama they all turned her life into. At least they were right about the last part.

"Where's AJ?" All the fussing made her restless.

"He's getting ready as well, sweetheart. You won't see him again until the ceremony. It's bad luck."

Lani sighed. A hug from AJ would really calm her nerves right now. She wasn't anxious about the marriage itself, or even becoming an official monarch, just ready to get all the official drama out of the way. Although the king usually did the speaking during the ceremony, AJ had suggested that she should say the words, too, to symbolize their equality as monarchs. Of course he was right and it was for the best, but what if she froze and forgot her words in front of all those people?

The sound of her phone made her jump. It took her

a while to find it on the dressing table amongst all the lotions and potions. Even her own hand—nails and fingertips decorated with red berry juice—startled her as she reached for it. "Hello?"

"How's my beautiful bride?" AJ's low voice, relaxed as always, made warmth flood her tense muscles.

"Nervous but okay. How's my handsome husband-to-be?"

"I'll be better when we're alone tonight." His suggestive tone made desire and anticipation trickle through her. Which was funny, really, since they'd slept together every night since he came back. "And the crowns are off our heads again."

"I know just how you feel." What a relief to have a partner she could really talk to. "I feel like we're participating in a costume party of some kind, not a real coronation."

AJ chuckled. "It is a costume party, complete with crowns woven from rare orchids and real gold. All we really have to do is smile and look regal. You've had more practice than I have."

"I wasn't very good at it. I've always felt like a milkmaid who'd stumbled into the palace and been mistaken for a princess."

"Easy to see how that could happen, with your looks."

Lani laughed. "How do you always manage to make me smile?"

"Because you love me, so you laugh, even at my worst jokes."

"I guess that must be it." She sighed. Her chest felt so full. "I do love you. I never thought I'd know real love, especially after I realized I wouldn't find it in my first marriage. What a surprise."

"There's really nothing better than a surprise when you least expect it—at least that was always my chief theory as a director."

"I'm not sure the citizens of Rahiri will feel the same way." She lifted a brow, then realized he couldn't see it over the phone. "They might prefer easy predictability."

"Then we'll try not to declare too many wars or set off too many loud explosions. Your gentle spirit will be a moderating influence on me."

"Maybe it will." She smiled. It was so easy and fun to tease AJ. "Though some might say my spirit is less gentle now it has you encouraging it into mischief."

"Mmm. I'm thinking about last night." AJ's throaty voice stirred heat deep inside her.

"We really should have saved our energy for today." Lani glanced at her glamorously made-up and gold-pollen-dusted visage in the mirror.

"Then we'd be more nervous. Much better to burn off some adrenaline first." AJ's voice slid into her ear, soft and seductive. "And even fresh pollen can't compete with the natural glow of a sexually satisfied woman."

"You're sending my thoughts in the wrong directions." Her pupils were dilating and her cheeks flushing an embarrassed pink. "Perhaps we need to turn our discussion to Rahiri's gross national product."

He laughed. "And how much it's growing due to the sale of souvenirs and tchotchkes associated with our nuptials. Speaking of which, it's almost time to head for the throne room. Try not to think about what we got up to in there when there weren't any crowds around."

Lani sucked in a breath. Would she be able to keep her mind focused on the age-old ceremony when she knew what they'd done on the surface of that ancient stone? "See you there, if I don't pass out from nerves on my way."

"You'll do just fine, your majesty."

Lani smiled as she ended the call. With AJ at her side, anything was possible.

Epilogue

Three years later

"It's lucky we have a home theater," Lani exclaimed, after AJ's umpteenth attempt to catch little Puaiti and return her to one of the velvet armchairs. Within seconds she'd popped up again like a jack-in-the-box and was running around the darkened room.

The credits for *Dragon Chaser 6: The Unveiling* were already scrolling on the screen.

"Yes, she doesn't seem to find the series too riveting," said AJ. He reached out to tickle her as she ran past. "But I suppose she's a bit outside our ideal demographic."

"She'd have a fit if you tried to leave her out." Priia chucked Puaiti's chin as she darted past her seat. "Always has to be at the center of the action, just like her dad."

She looked fondly at AJ. They all knew that in Priia's mind, AJ, not Vanu, who was rarely mentioned, was Puaiti's father.

Apparently Puaiti took after AJ in every way except gender, including a passion for movies, though now, at age three, the Disney princesses were her favorites. She sported a yellow Sleeping Beauty gown as she leapt onto AJ's lap and begged for more popcorn.

Her baby sister, Maya, slept in Lani's arms. She could sleep through almost anything, which was lucky with Puaiti around.

"Ray did a great job. I don't think I could have done better." He gave Puaiti a piece of popcorn and watched carefully while she ate it. Lani had explained that popcorn was a choking hazard and AJ, attentive father that he was, took the warning seriously.

"I think you might have made the chase scene on the bridge a touch more dramatic." Lani stroked Maya's silky golden hair. "I suspect you might have added an aerial component involving the suspension cables."

AJ stared at her, humor glittering in his eyes. "How did you know that's exactly what I was thinking?"

"Well, I have seen your films a few times." She glanced at Priia. "Along with your greatest fan."

Priia dusted popcorn salt off her hands. "My AJ would have made the film very exciting, but he's more valuable here in Rahiri."

"Don't you miss your shopping trips to Rodeo Drive, Mom?" AJ leaned toward her. "You don't have any good excuse to fly all the way to L.A. to shop anymore."

"Sweetheart, thanks to you and your tourism initiatives, I don't need to. There's going to be a Chanel and a Fendi opening right here in the new visitors' village." She leaned toward Lani and lifted a penciled brow. "Possibly a Ferragamo, too, but that's not definite yet."

Lani smiled. "I'm looking forward to the new JoJo Maman Bébé. Maya told me she'd like some designer diapers." She winked at AJ. They both enjoyed teasing Priia about her passion for luxury labels. No one could argue that the visitors now streaming to the island brought funds to build schools, hospitals and other services that would have been unimaginable a generation ago.

"Smart girl." Priia held out her arms. "Why don't you give her to me and go enjoy the sunset. I know our littlest princess has been keeping you busy around the clock all week. Puaiti and I will read Maya a story, won't we, Puaiti?"

The toddler pulled a book from her stash near the video controls. "She loves Winnie the Pooh!"

AJ slipped his hand into hers and the familiar thrill danced up her arm. They walked out onto the veranda as Priia recited the opening lines of *The House at Pooh Corner,* for probably the seventieth time.

The sun was setting over the valley below and she could just make out the roar of the waterfall under the animated hum of the evening chorus. The soft copper light animated AJ's handsome features. She could swear he'd become even more gorgeous—as well as more dignified—since he'd assumed the role of king. The commentators on *Celebrity Watch* had recently made the same observation, much to AJ's amusement.

"Are you sleepy?" AJ stroked her cheek.

"Not in the least." Her body hummed with fresh energy and she wrapped her arms around her husband's waist. A shiver of anticipation made her lips tingle for a split second before they kissed. "Maybe we should sneak off to the throne room and lock the door so no one could disturb us?"

AJ's dark eyes smoldered with familiar passion. "I like the way you think."

* * * * *

COMING NEXT MONTH

Available May 10, 2011

#2083 KING'S MILLION-DOLLAR SECRET
Maureen Child
Kings of California

#2084 EXPOSED: HER UNDERCOVER MILLIONAIRE
Michelle Celmer
The Takeover

#2085 SECRET SON, CONVENIENT WIFE
Maxine Sullivan
Billionaires and Babies

#2086 TEXAS-SIZED TEMPTATION
Sara Orwig
Stetsons & CEOs

#2087 DANTE'S HONOR-BOUND HUSBAND
Day Leclaire
The Dante Legacy

#2088 CARRYING THE RANCHER'S HEIR
Charlene Sands

> You can find more information on upcoming
> Harlequin® titles, free excerpts and more at
> **www.HarlequinInsideRomance.com.**

HDCNM0411

REQUEST YOUR FREE BOOKS!

2 FREE NOVELS PLUS 2 FREE GIFTS!

ALWAYS POWERFUL, PASSIONATE AND PROVOCATIVE

*With an evil force hell-bent on destruction,
two enemies must unite to find a truth that turns
all-too-personal when passions collide.*

*Enjoy a sneak peek in Jenna Kernan's next installment
in her original* TRACKER *series, GHOST STALKER,
available in May, only from Harlequin Nocturne.*

"Who are you?" he snarled.

Jessie lifted her chin. "Your better."

His smile was cold. "Such arrogance could only come from a Niyanoka."

She nodded. "Why are you here?"

"I don't know." He glanced about her room. "I asked the birds to take me to a healer."

"And they have done so. Is that *all* you asked?"

"No. To lead them away from my friends." His eyes fluttered and she saw them roll over white.

Jessie straightened, preparing to flee, but he roused himself and mastered the momentary weakness. His eyes snapped open, locking on her.

Her heart hammered as she inched back.

"Lead who away?" she whispered, suddenly afraid of the answer.

"The ghosts. Nagi sent them to attack me so I would bring them to her."

The wolf must be deranged because Nagi did not send ghosts to attack living creatures. He captured the evil ones after their death if they refused to walk the Way of Souls, forcing them to face judgment.

"Her? The healer you seek is also female?"

"Michaela. She's Niyanoka, like you. The last Seer of Souls and Nagi wants her dead."

Jessie fell back to her seat on the carpet as the possibility of this ricocheted in her brain. Could it be true?

"Why should I believe you?" But she knew why. His black aura, the part that said he had been touched by death. Only a ghost could do that. But it made no sense.

Why would Nagi hunt one of her people and why would a Skinwalker want to protect her? She had been trained from birth to hate the Skinwalkers, to consider them a threat.

His intent blue eyes pinned her. Jessie felt her mouth go dry as she considered the impossible. Could the trickster be speaking the truth? Great Mystery, what evil was this?

She stared in astonishment. There was only one way to find her answers. But she had never even met a Skinwalker before and so did not even know if they dreamed.

But if he dreamed, she would have her chance to learn the truth.

*Look for GHOST STALKER by Jenna Kernan,
available May only from Harlequin Nocturne,
wherever books and ebooks are sold.*

SAME GREAT STORIES AND AUTHORS!

Starting April 2011,
Silhouette Desire will become
Harlequin Desire, but rest assured
that this series will continue to be
the ultimate destination for Powerful,
Passionate and Provocative Romance
with the same great authors that
you've come to know and love!

Harlequin

Desire

ALWAYS POWERFUL, PASSIONATE
AND PROVOCATIVE

Fan favorite author
TINA LEONARD
is back with
an exciting new miniseries.

Six bachelor brothers are given a challenge—
get married, start a big family and whoever does
so first will inherit the famed Rancho Diablo.
Too bad none of these cowboys is marriage material!

> ## *Callahan Cowboys:*
> ### Catch one if you can!

The Cowboy's Triplets (May 2011)
The Cowboy's Bonus Baby (July 2011)
The Bull Rider's Twins (Sept 2011)
Bonus Callahan Christmas Novella! (Nov 2011)
His Valentine Triplets (Jan 2012)
Cowboy Sam's Quadruplets (March 2012)
A Callahan Wedding (May 2012)